UZ

Short Story
COLLECTION

~

UMM ZAKIYYAH

UZ Short Story Collection
By Umm Zakiyyah

ISBN: 978-1-942985-04-4
Library of Congress Control Number: 2016932830

Order information available online at
uzauthor.com
ummzakiyyah.com/store

Verses from Qur'an taken from Saheeh International, Darussalam, and
Yusuf Ali translations.

Published by Al-Walaa Publications
Camp Springs, Maryland USA

For the latest by Umm Zakiyyah, visit

UZauthor.com

"You can't rush healing, and you can't rush triumph. Inherent in both is the need for patience and perseverance. And each takes time."

—from the journal of Umm Zakiyyah

Glossary of Arabic Terms

Allah: the Arabic term for "God"

'abeed: derogatory term derived from the Arabic word meaning *slave*, often used to denigrate a person with black or brown skin

As-salaamu'alaikum: the Muslim greeting of peace, literally "peace be upon you," often said in place of "hello" and "goodbye."

da'wah: any teaching about Islam for the purpose of clarifying religious misunderstandings or inviting someone to become Muslim

du'aa: informal prayer or supplication to God

fitnah: trial, tribulation, or something that causes great difficulty to face or overcome

Fus-ha: classical Arabic (as opposed to colloquial)

haraam: forbidden, sinful

inshaaAllah or *insha'Allah:* God-willing or if God wills

Istikhaarah: formal prayer and supplication performed when trying to make a decision about something when a person is uncertain what is best

jilbaab: outer garment for Muslim women that resembles a large, loose dress, sometimes used in reference to the all-black Saudi-style abaya that extends from the top of the head to the floor

khimaar: cloth head cover worn by Muslim women, often referred to as hijab

maasha Allah or *mashaAllah:* "It was God's will," often expressed in admiration of something or in acceptance of something that has happened

madhhab: an Islamic school of thought

nasheeds: songs with no musical instrument accompaniment

niqaab: face veil

Qur'an: the Muslim holy book

shahaadah or *shahādah:* formal testimony recited to mark one's entry into Islam: "I bear witness that nothing has the right to be worshipped except God alone and that Muhammad is His prophet and messenger."

subhaan Allah: expression of glorification of God, often uttered in surprise or excitement about something

wali: a woman's marriage guardian

Wallah: a term used to make an oath in God's name, often uttered to underscore the sincerity or importance of what is being said

TABLE OF CONTENTS
SHORT STORIES BY UMM ZAKIYYAH

The Arranged Marriage

a short story

Mohsina, daughter of Muslim immigrants to America, is a college student who is very vocal in her arguments against her professor's anti-Islam rhetoric about Muslim women being forced into unwanted marriages...until her parents try to force her into an unwanted marriage.

~

UMM ZAKIYYAH

To anyone else, today was an ordinary day, even if a bit dreary. The ground was wet from a fresh rain. The brown-green blades of grass glistened despite their imminent death. Dirt blotched the untended grass in patches, making Mohsina think of the back of her father's head. His ever-growing bald spot, the color of aged chocolate like the rest of him, often made Mohsina think of the shameful bareness she felt whenever she walked into her social-psychology class. The professor grunted every time. And it stung every time. Though she was never quite sure if the sound of unambiguous disapproval was because she was suddenly present or because he was suddenly upset at the moment she was present. But it made her tug uncomfortably at her plain, black shoulder abaya and run a hand self-consciously over the cloth of her off-white hijab, like her father would run his calloused fingers over that bald spot whenever he was nervous or painfully self-aware all of a sudden.

"*Bah*," Dr. Sherman would say in terse annoyance as he flapped his hand dismissively at Mohsina's insistent, even if meek, protests against his Islamophobic tirades.

"It's not because of Islam that so many Muslim women suffer," she would blurt out before he gave her permission to speak. She feared if she waited for him to notice her reluctantly raised hand and point to her, she wouldn't be able to say anything in response, not only because the gray-haired professor was bigoted and closed-minded, but also because Mohsina herself might lose the nerve. "Islam doesn't allow men to enslave girls and sell them as virtual sex slaves into unwanted marriages."

"You are naïve," Dr. Sherman would say in a tone so subdued that Mohsina would squirm and look away from him. "You have no idea what you're talking about."

"I'm Muslim," she would say, her voice shaking as she tried to speak more loudly, more confidently. "I should know."

"Yes you should," he would say. "But you don't." Then he would look at her, eyes squinted from beneath the bushy gray-brown of his eyebrows. "Where is your family from again?"

Mohsina would swallow hard and avert her gaze. She hated this question. It was almost rhetorical. It was a cruel, even if subtle, announcement to all her white- and brown-skinned "real" American classmates that she was inauthentic, an imposter. She was born in America and held a blue passport just like they did.

Why should she be put on the spot? *"Where is* your *family from?"* she wanted to ask the pale-skinned, blue-eyed professor with dirty blond hair and an overflowing beard; the almond-skinned, dark brown-eyed girl with braids plaited to her scalp and who always kept an iPod hidden on her lap; the tanned, used-to-be-white-skinned redhead who annoyingly picked at the blackheads on her chin—and the rest of the arrogant "Americans" who studied in furtive glances Mohsina's creamy-coffee complexion and ebony eyes, and could only guess at the length and texture of Mohsina's dark black hair tucked and hidden beneath the ubiquitous hijab.

No, Mohsina's parents had not been Americans when their international flight landed in New York twenty years ago. They had been armed only with student visas and pathetic hopes and dreams for something better than "back home" (though that "something better" remained an elusive, if not mysterious, concept to their daughter even nineteen years after her birth only miles from the Statue of Liberty, a birth that allegedly represented the bulk of that "something better").

Mohsina's parents had exchanged the student visas for work visas and the work visas for green cards and the green cards for the coveted blue passports. But their only mistake, in Mohsina's view, was exchanging their student-work-green idealism for the bitter reality they inadvertently signed their children up for even before they were born.

But, yes, Mohsina's parents were American, just like the families of these snobby students, whose parents' parents' great grandparents likely arrived in a less flattering mode of transport than Mohsina's, though with painstakingly similarly stupid ideas and tragic realities, the former or latter description most fitting depending on whether they arrived in the upper or lower deck.

"Why does it matter? Where we're from?" Mohsina would manage to say in response to the professor's never-ending question that challenged the validity of her nationality, the validity of her existence. And she knew her voice was shaking, but her hand was also trembling, and she didn't like that. She hated that, actually. She hated that she let these self-righteous people get to her. "It shouldn't matter. It *doesn't* matter."

"It should matter, and it *does* matter," Dr. Sherman would say before going on with his tirade as if Mohsina hadn't interrupted him at all, as if Mohsina wasn't sitting there at all, as if Mohsina didn't exist at all.

The dull rubber heal of Mohsina's shoe sank low into a patch of mud she didn't see after she had stepped over another. She pulled her foot up carefully and frowned only briefly as she glanced down to see that the dark brown muck had risen over the sides of her slip-on shoe and soiled a thick white sock. *At least it's only one foot ruined*, she thought to herself as she pulled at her heavy book bag and readjusted it on her shoulder.

A cold wetness plopped on the tip of her nose, and Mohsina instinctively swatted at it, inadvertently scratching the skin of her upper lip. When three more, then five more plopped on her cheeks, it became obvious to her that it was only rain. She looked up, her mouth agape as she shielded her eyes from the bright blur peering behind the darkening clouds. Her face was slapped with at least a dozen more, as if punishment for becoming annoyed in the first place. She turned her gaze back to the path in front of her and swallowed the drops that had fallen on her tongue, surprised by their sweet, salty taste.

"We are not like these selfish, reckless people," her mother had told her a month before. "We don't marry for love. We don't marry for our own foolish desires. We marry for our families. We marry for our cultures. We marry for

Allah." Her mother had said the Creator's name with such determined emphasis that Mohsina almost believed her. A pang of guilt had stabbed Mohsina, and she felt ashamed of herself. Who was she to choose love? Who was she to have foolish desires? Who was she to disrespect her family, insult her culture, and turn away from Allah?

"But he's Muslim," Mohsina had said, her voice a cross between an unabashed plea and a pathetic whine. "Can't you just consider him? How is that selfish?"

The slap was so quick, so intense that Mohsina just stood still, blinking in disbelief as the solid white wall behind her mother's angry, contorted face seemed to tip to one side.

"Who are you to question your parents?" her mother shot back, apparently unaware that Mohsina was struggling to overcome dizziness. "Do you know how much dowry he is paying us for you? Do you have any *idea*?"

Islam doesn't allow men to enslave girls and sell them as virtual sex slaves into unwanted marriages.

"Or are you so drunk with all these stupid American ideas that you've forgotten who you are, where we come from?"

Why does it matter? Where we're from?

"You are nothing without your family. You are nothing without your culture. You are nothing without your *honor*."

It shouldn't matter. It doesn't *matter.*

This morning, Mohsina had turned off her cell phone and left it on the bus that rounded the college campus and on its fifth stop dropped her off in front of the tall, daunting, brick humanities building in which Dr. Sherman taught. As she wiped her muddied shoe against the concrete of the sidewalk that early, dreary morning, Mohsina wondered if Dr. Sherman would grunt at exactly 7:58, the time she usually walked into class.

The rain came down harder and soaked the sleeves of her abaya, but it was the clothes beneath—and in her book bag—that she was most worried about. But Mohsina had been standing on the corner behind the university parking garage for only two minutes when the familiar car pulled up and slowed to a stop beside her, its windshield wipers working furiously against the pouring rain.

She opened the passenger-side door and got in without a word and only mumbled her reply to the salaams. Sadness tugged at her heart as she considered what she was giving up by shutting that car door, pulling the seatbelt around her, and snapping it firmly in place.

It should matter, and it does *matter.*

Oddly, this made her smile, just a bit. She would miss her bigoted professor and her father's bald spot and her mother's uneven temper. But she would write them, maybe a year later, when this was all over and their hearts could only remember the good, when they would wish they could do it all over again and hear her, really hear their daughter when she spoke to them.

In the letter, Mohsina planned in her head, she'd say, "Thank you."

Yes, she'd say, "Thank you." And why not?

She would say kind words, just like the ones in Mohsina's favorite song "Thank You for Hearing Me" by Sinead O'Connor.

> *Thank you, thank you for helping me*
> *Thank you for breaking my heart*
> *Thank you for tearing me apart*
> *Now I've a strong, strong heart*

But by then—Mohsina let herself imagine life beyond the rushed ceremony with the sympathetic American imam whom her parents refused to even talk to because he wasn't from their country—she would probably have a bundle of new life in her arms (a son, maybe a daughter, it didn't matter) whom she could present as a peace offering, as their own flesh and blood, to say, "See? It does matter. It *should* matter."

Tears filled her eyes at this thought, but she let herself imagine the shock on her parents' faces after they learned of Mohsina's own "arranged marriage." It would have been identical to the one they had planned for her, except this one had been arranged by Mohsina herself—with the support of her future husband and some "real" American Muslims—and after a zillion failed attempts at diplomacy with her own family, who coupled their self-righteousness with not the least bit of respect for what Allah really said marriage was supposed to be.

"Why did you choose America, of all places?" Mohsina had asked, exasperated after a particularly rough day of anti-Muslim bullying when she was in middle school.

"We couldn't live back home anymore," her father had told her, distant sadness in his eyes. "Times were tough, and it was destroying us. We had to take a chance and start life over again. We wanted better for ourselves. We wanted better for our future children."

Mohsina wiped the unfallen tears from her eyes and leaned back in the passenger seat and exhaled in a single breath. It felt good to know that her father already understood, even if he didn't know it just yet—and wouldn't know it fully until Mohsina herself reappeared with the "blue passport" of her life firmly in her hands.

Pretending To Obey Allah

a short story

Hakimah tries to convince a defiant student that struggling with wearing hijab is not hypocrisy.

~

UMM ZAKIYYAH

"No," Amatullah said shaking her head, folding her arms across her chest defiantly as she leaned back in her chair. "I'm not going to cover just because you asked me to."

Hakimah sighed from where she sat on a desk opposite the student she had taught for four years, her thoughts drifting momentarily. Her gaze rested on the row of windows at the back of the tenth grade classroom. Distant sounds of students laughing and running and talking could be heard through the glass, underscoring the vast distance between her and her student.

Perhaps it wasn't a good idea to have asked Amatullah to stay after class. Hakimah wasn't sure. But her heart could not rest until she at least made an effort.

"But, Amatullah," Hakimah said softly, her eyes now on Amatullah who refused to look at her. Amatullah's face showed obvious resentment toward Hakimah for causing her to miss spending break with friends. "It's Ramadan. Don't you think it's a good time to start?"

There was a brief silence before Amatullah narrowed her eyes toward Hakimah, and that's when Hakimah noticed the tears glistening in her student's eyes.

"What for?" Amatullah's tone was accusatory and defensive. "I don't want to be a hypocrite like these other girls."

Hakimah furrowed her brows. "A hypocrite?"

Amatullah rolled her eyes. It was obvious she didn't want to have this conversation. "You see them," she shot back. "They're always walking around all covered up, but they're no better than anybody else."

"Who thinks they're better than everyone else?"

"All of 'em." Amatullah gestured toward the window behind her. "And they do the same things I do. But at least I don't claim to be someone I'm not." She folded her arms on her chest again, shaking her head.

"I can't believe you fall for it," Amatullah vented. "And you think you know so much about Islam. You don't know half the things that go on with these so-called religious girls."

Hakimah drew in a deep breath, a bit offended by the comment. But it wasn't the first time she'd heard it. Moments like this she wondered if she'd made the right decision coming to work as an Islamic studies teacher at the only Muslim school in her city. Islamic studies wasn't her specialty, but she did try to make the class interesting by doing things like giving each lesson its own title; the last one had been "Making the Most out of Ramadan." Sometimes she'd let the students choose the lesson title; other times she'd choose it herself. It was her way of giving them a sense of ownership, something she'd learned to do for clients while studying counseling for her master's.

When Hakimah had applied for work at the private Islamic academy four years ago, she was applying for a position as a biology teacher, the same position she'd held at a public school at her last job. She already knew she'd suffer a huge pay cut, but after facing repeated racial and religious discrimination at the middle school that catered mainly to the middle and upper class residents who lived near the school, Hakimah decided it was time to move on. Besides, the political tug-of-war with the administration, staff, and parents was taking a toll on her health, and her faith. Hakimah was Muslim when they hired her, but it was only in the last two years of working there that she had made the difficult decision to wear hijab to work. That's when everything changed...

"Amatullah," Hakimah said, exhaling as she was reminded of her own confusion before making the decision to cover full time, "it's not fair to call your friends hypocrites. They're Muslim just like you."

"If you knew the things they do, I think you'd call them hypocrites too."

Hakimah shook her head. "I don't think I would, Amatullah, no matter what I knew. Anyway," she sighed, "I didn't ask you to stay after to talk about them. I want to talk about you."

Amatullah grew quiet, but her defiance remained. She shook her head at some private thought that disturbed her, but she said nothing.

"I'm just asking you to think about what I said." Hakimah hoped her sincere concern showed in her voice. But she wasn't sure. "Ramadan is a time for changes. It's a time to look at your life and see what you can do differently."

The room grew quiet momentarily.

Hakimah wasn't sure what else she should say, or if she should say anything else at all. "I know it's a hard decision, Amatullah. Believe me, I know, but—"

"Ms. Khan," Amatullah interrupted, "I know you think you're helping and all. But I already know who I am and what I need to do. And I'm not going to cover now, even if it's Ramadan."

"But why not, Amatullah? Allah promises th—"

"What's the point of covering if I'm just going to take it off later?" Amatullah rolled her eyes and shook her head. "Like I said, I'm not a hypocrite. When I'm ready to cover, I'll do it all the time. But I'll do it for Allah, not because some *teacher* asked me to."

"But even if you do take it off later, Amatullah, Allah is forgiving and merciful. You can—"

"Why would I even *do* something like that?" Amatullah wrinkled her nose.

"I'm not saying you *plan* to take it off later," Hakimah corrected herself, realizing how her last comment sounded. "I'm just saying if you get weak, you can always ask for strength. Allah will be there for you. You just have to put in the effort."

"But why would I *pretend*?"

Hakimah creased her forehead, taken aback by the question. "What do you mean?"

"If I'm not strong enough to cover all the time, I shouldn't cover."

"But, Amatullah, you can't *pretend* to obey Allah. If you're obeying Allah, you're obeying Allah, even if you make mistakes sometimes."

"Can I go now?" Amatullah's nose flared as she met Hakimah's eyes unblinking. The sounds of other student's laughter rose near the windows.

Hakimah drew in a deep breath and exhaled, reminded that break would be over soon. She had a class next period. "Yes, you may go if you—"

Amatullah's chair screeched as she quickly stood, throwing her book bag over her shoulder, not waiting to hear what Hakimah had to say. Seconds later, Amatullah was out the door, and the door closed behind her.

For a minute, Hakimah remained in her place, her eyes staring beyond Amatullah's empty chair to the recess area beyond the windows. Amatullah, now outside, appeared several feet from the glass. Her profile displayed a wide grin as her friends approached to give her a hug. A moment later, Amatullah laughed at something a friend whispered to her, her voice reverberating in the classroom.

But why would I pretend?

Hakimah was reminded of a conversation she'd had with a former coworker after she started wearing hijab regularly. "The problem with you Muslims is you think your clothes make you pious," the man had said. "For you, it's all about image. For us, it's all about faith."

At the time, Hakimah had been so offended that she wasn't sure if her response did her religion, or herself, any justice. She remembered saying something about hijab not being about image and how actions proved a person's faith, but now she realized where the real confusion lay.

In the heart.

That was the missing piece.

But why would I pretend?

With a sincere heart, you wouldn't. Because pretending simply wouldn't be possible. And obeying Allah wouldn't be a decision you have to make. It would be the natural reflection of the sincerity in your heart.

The bell rang, and the noise level near the window rose as students scrambled back into the building, laughing and talking as they passed the glass. Inspired suddenly, Hakimah stood and walked over to her desk, where she sat down and jotted down some notes for her next class.

She already knew what its title would be: "Pretending to Obey Allah: Is it Even Possible?"

The
Muslim
Girl

a short story

Inaya faces an identity crisis after her family moves back to America and she must wear hijab in public school.

~

UMM
ZAKIYYAH

When my mother became Muslim, I didn't even know what a Muslim was. I mean, what does a nine-year-old know about religion?

I remember when she first told me. I was tucking the Ebony *magazine under my pillow so that my parents wouldn't know I was reading it. I looked up and saw my mother standing near my bedroom door. Her arms were folded, and she was frowning, looking all upset. I thought she was angry with me for reading "grown-up stuff," but she just sat on the edge of my bed and smiled at me.*

"Naya, I'm Muslim now." Her eyes seemed sad for some reason.

"What?"

"I'm Muslim." Her smile seemed childlike, like she was waiting for my approval.

I averted my gaze and pulled the covers up to my shoulders as I settled under them. "Okay." I had no idea what she was talking about, but since I was pretty sure I wasn't in trouble, I just wanted to go to sleep.

My mother stood and patted my head. "Thanks, Naya." She turned off the light and closed the door as she left. I lay awake in the darkness for several minutes before finally shutting my eyes and drifting to sleep.

"Children are resilient." That's what my father used to say. Maybe that's why I jumped head-on into Islam myself and even learned Arabic and Qur'an and thought it was "cool" to live in Saudi Arabia.

Oh my God.

Did I really think that?

Saudi Arabia

"Surprise!"

Inaya's eyes widened as she surveyed the large room that was filled with dozens of girls she had met during the seven years she had lived in Riyadh. Amongst them were Saudi girls she had tutored in English or met at school, as well as expats from India, Pakistan, America, and the United Kingdom whom she had befriended or met during an Arabic or Qur'an class.

Inaya laughed and glanced behind her at her mother, and Veronica grinned back at Inaya, the baby against Veronica's chest from where she stood in the doorway of the small house. The rest of the women, mothers of most of the girls, relaxed outside on blankets spread out on grass patches atop the dirt and sand. The expansive land was enclosed by a tall stone wall that afforded the women maximum privacy when they removed their abayas and veils.

"The first thing I want to say, Inaya, is that you're an inspiration to all of us, *maasha Allah*." The Saudi girls who had been singing and playing the drum now stood in front of the room as the other girls sat on the Arab-style floor couch that lined the room's walls, looking at the sisters as the elder one spoke. Tears glistened in Batool's eyes as she gazed at Inaya.

"I'm really sad to see you go," Batool said, "*Wallah*, before I met you, I took the Qur'an for granted. And I took Arabic for granted too. But seeing you memorize the whole Qur'an and push everyone to learn Arabic, *subhaan Allah*, it made me realize how important Qur'an and *Fus-ha* should be in our lives."

Batool's younger sister nodded her head, her expression thoughtful.

"I remember when I first met you," Batool said, smiling sadly, "and I asked why you want to learn Arabic when you already have the best language in the world."

Inaya smiled at the memory, bowing her head from where she sat next to Rafa on the floor couch, a half-eaten plate of food on the carpet by her feet.

"And you said, 'No, *you* have the best language in the world. What can be better than the language of Qur'an?'"

Batool shook her head as she drew in a deep breath. "*Wallah*, hearing you say that made me so ashamed, and after that I started memorizing Qur'an myself."

***

We have no idea what we're going to do without you,
"The girl who gets things done."
But I suppose we'll have to figure out a way to still learn, Do things right, and have some fun!
Thanks for teaching us the meaning of friendship
And love for Allah's sake.
Thanks for telling us to pray and cover—
Without taking a break!
Thanks for teaching us that Islam is a religion of action, Not a religion of words.
Thanks for reminding us that saying
No! to Allah (about anything) is absurd.
We're going to miss you, Inaya,
Our beloved sister, "cousin", and friend.
But like you always say, "Keep the faith, girl,
And, insha'Allah, we'll meet in the End."

Inaya smiled as she sat on the edge of her bed late that night, re-reading the poem the girls had written and given to her. A second later Inaya thought of her father and friends in America, and Inaya's heart swelled in anticipation for her flight back home next week.

America

"Are you going to wear those Arab clothes to school every day?"

It took a moment for Inaya to register her Christian cousin's question. Inaya creased her forehead and sat up, her hands now in her lap. "What?"

"Those black robes." Kayla gestured her head toward the chair where Inaya's *khimaar* and *jilbaab* hung over its back. "Will you wear them to school?"

Inaya contorted her face in offense. "Yes."

"Chill," Kayla said, her lip upturned. "I was just curious."

Inaya rolled her eyes. What was Kayla getting at? That Inaya's clothes were ugly or something? Kayla saw Inaya every day at school. They even had English class together. So Kayla knew that Inaya would wear the clothes to school because Inaya had already worn them to school—every day.

"I just don't get it, that's all."

"Get what?" Inaya glared at Kayla defensively.

"Why you dress like that."

"I'm Muslim, Kayla. Quit trying to act stupid."

Kayla narrowed her eyes at her cousin. "Girl, what's your problem? I didn't know Muslims had to dress like somebody died."

Inaya widened her eyes, wounded. "I'm not dressing like somebody died. I'm dressing like a Muslim."

"Then why doesn't Nasra dress like you?"

Inaya grew quiet. Nasra was a senior at the school and was well-liked despite being openly Muslim, at least that's the impression Inaya got.

Inaya had met Nasra on Thursday during lunch period when Nasra had come to the table where Inaya was sitting with Kayla and her friends. After handing them a flyer about her campaign for Student Council, Nasra shared what she planned to do if she were elected president.

But Inaya remembered nothing of what Nasra had said. Inaya couldn't get over how Nasra spoke to her classmates as if she were their equal, as if she wasn't wearing a cloth draped around her head and neck and an oversized shirt that hung to the knees of her baggy jeans. Nasra had even given Inaya salaams before she left to the next lunch table.

But Inaya had averted her gaze and mumbled a reply, fearing her schoolmates would overhear and think she was weird for speaking a foreign language.

"Nasra is different," Inaya said, her voice tight with emotion. She hoped her cousin would change the subject.

Kayla squinted her eyes curiously. "But aren't you both Muslim?"

Inaya had no idea what to say. "Yeah, but…" But what?

"Why don't you just dress like Nasra?" Kayla said. "Then you wouldn't look so drab."

Inaya groaned and rolled her eyes.

Abdullah started to squirm and whine in his car seat.

"No offense," Kayla said.

"Just forget it," Inaya said as she shoved herself off the bed and kneeled next to her little brother. "It doesn't matter anyway."

But it did matter, Inaya thought. The deadweight of dread hung in her chest as she rocked her little brother's chair back and forth to quiet his cries. She had no idea how she would stomach walking into school Monday morning wearing the same "drab" black *khimaar* and *jilbaab* she had worn all last week.

School

Inaya's heart raced wildly as she shrugged off her *jilbaab* and walked toward the full-size mirror in the girls' restroom, where a few students were applying make-up. Knowing her mother would be upset, Inaya felt guilty for taking off her *jilbaab*, but she balled up the garment and stuffed it into her book bag. *At least I'm still wearing my hijab*, she thought to herself.

The reflection in the mirror startled Inaya. Her appearance was in stark contrast to her growing insecurity. The white blouse and skirt fell loosely over Inaya's form but accented her shape so attractively that it was breathtaking.

Is that me?

Inaya's body jerked as someone yanked on her arm, the motion causing the *khimaar* to loosen itself from her head.

"You go girl!" Kayla said, a wide grin on her face. She squeezed Inaya's arm approvingly as she looked Inaya up and down. "That really suits you."

Inaya smiled despite herself as she reached up to readjust her hijab. "You think so?"

Kayla nodded emphatically. "Definitely."

Inaya was still smiling as she tucked a piece of black fabric under her chin, but the *khimaar* did not stay in place. Groaning, Inaya pulled the cloth from her head then carefully set it back on her head. A few braids escaped from the elastic ponytail holder, making it impossible to readjust the head cover without re-securing the elastic band. Inaya sighed and draped the cloth over her shoulders so she could fix her hair.

"I'm glad you gave up that—"

The shrilling of the bell interrupted Kayla midsentence, and her eyes widened in fear. "Oh my God," Kayla said. The other students scrambled out the bathroom, shoving roughly past Kayla and Inaya. "That's the second bell."

Inaya's heart raced as she fumbled with the band at the back of her head. She didn't want to be late, but if she didn't leave now with Kayla, she probably would be. Inaya was still learning her way around the large school, and she doubted she could find her class on her own.

"Come on." Kayla's eyes pleaded, annoyance on her face. "We only have a minute before they give late passes."

Inaya quickly tucked her braids into a small bun then reached for the *khimaar* that was draped over her shoulders. When she didn't feel the cloth immediately, she looked down at herself then at her reflection. The fabric was nowhere in sight.

"What?" Kayla's voice became concerned all of a sudden.

"My hijab—" Frantic, Inaya patted herself and looked at her reflection again.

"Your *what*?"

"M-m-my..." Inaya was so panicked she couldn't speak. A hand went to her head as her eyes scanned the floor near where she stood.

It took Kayla only a second to register what her cousin was looking for, and she too turned and started to look for the cloth.

"Can't you just find it later?"

A surge of anger rose in Inaya's chest, and she started to respond flippantly. But her thoughts were interrupted as she saw a flash of black peeking from behind the wall leading to the restroom exit.

Inaya rushed toward it, but she withdrew her hand and halted her steps when she saw that the *khimaar* was trampled with shoeprints and lay next to an overflowing trashcan. A small puddle of dirty water glistened from beneath the fabric, and a discarded paper towel lay crumpled atop.

"There it is," Kayla said, sighing in relief as she grabbed the *khimaar* from the floor and shoved it into Inaya's hand. "Now let's go."

Kayla pulled Inaya by the arm, and Inaya shuffled her feet as she reluctantly followed her cousin.

Inaya felt naked beneath the bright fluorescent lights of the wide hallway as Kayla quickened her steps and let go of Inaya's arm. Inaya fell back and dragged her feet, letting the gap between her and her cousin grow wider.

"Your class is right around the corner upstairs," Kayla called out over her shoulder.

"See you at lunch," Kayla said before she broke into a sprint toward her own classroom.

But Inaya's thoughts were not on being late to class. As she slowly approached the staircase, her eyes were on the soiled *khimaar* balled up in her hand.

She needed to put on her hijab. The urgency of the thought made Inaya glance back at the bathroom as she mentally calculated how long it would take to clean the cloth and put it back on.

Maybe she should just skip homeroom, she considered. That way she'd have time to get properly dressed.

But the cold dampness of the fabric repulsed her. Could she really put the filthy cloth back on her head, even if she washed it in the sink first?

"Get to class!" someone called out from down the hall.

What if I don't put it back on? Inaya thought to herself. *Then I can look normal like the other girls.*

What was she doing? Was she out of her mind?

For a moment, Inaya's legs felt as if they would give out. She halted her steps to lean against a wall, the throbbing in her head making her feel dizzy.

What if her mother found out? Or even her stepfather?

Thanks for teaching us…love for Allah's sake.

Thanks for telling us to pray and cover—
Without taking a break!

Inaya could almost hear Rafa and her friends reciting the poem, their words an eerie taunt that traveled across a continent and an ocean to haunt Inaya at this moment.

Inaya dropped her head in shame and felt the deadweight of the black cloth that was stuffed into the bag slung over her shoulder.

Why didn't Inaya just wash it in the restroom and dry it with the automatic hand dryer?

No, she wasn't going to go through the trouble. Anyway, it wasn't her fault that the *khimaar* was completely ruined. And even if it were, there was nothing Inaya could do about it now.

Read *Muslim Girl*, the novel at uzauthor.com

The
Bad
Muslim

a short story

Tired of being judged harshly because she's an American convert to Islam, Joanne argues with her friend, Basma, about their different views on raising their daughters.

~

UMM
ZAKIYYAH

"I can't believe you let Maryam have internet in her room," Joanne said. She gripped the steering wheel of her car with her left hand as she lifted a can of diet cola from the cup holder and took a sip. She shook her head as she held the can inches from her mouth. "I swear that's the one thing that makes me really uncomfortable when Samira comes over."

In her peripheral vision, Joanne could see Basma turn to look at her, Basma's narrowed eyes visible through the slit in the black face veil, but Joanne kept her eyes on the road. She already knew what her friend was thinking. It was what most Muslims thought when they heard her views on teens and internet usage. It was the same frustration she'd faced in Saudi Arabia. If you didn't wear a face veil and you listened to music, you forfeited all rights to being taken seriously for any moral boundaries you set for yourself and your family. And fact that Joanne was an American convert to Islam made her case even worse.

"Really, Joanne," Basma said, shaking her head, "I'm surprised you feel that way."

"Why? Because I'm a bad Muslim and should just go all the way?" Joanne chuckled and shook her head before taking another sip of cola.

"I didn't say that."

"You didn't have to."

Joanne returned the can to its place and smiled at Basma.

"Don't worry," Joanne said. "I don't blame you for it. I'm used to people thinking I'm a hypocrite."

"Oh, Joanne, for God's sake. Can we talk about something else?"

"I didn't bring this up to bicker, Basma. I'm really worried about my daughter."

"And you don't think I'd treat her like my own?"

Joanne slowed the car to a stop behind a line of vehicles at a red light. "Honestly, Basma," she said quietly. "That's what I *don't* want you to do."

Joanne frowned apologetically as she met Basma's shocked gaze. "I'm sorry if it sounds like I'm being judgmental, but—"

"If anyone should be worried," Basma said, "it should be me."

Joanne's eyes widened as she chuckled. "And what's that supposed to mean?"

"It means you're not the only one worried about her daughter."

"So you believe Samira will corrupt your innocent little girl?" Joanne rolled her eyes and smirked. "I should've known this is what you'd think after I asked if our daughters could be friends. To you, this whole thing is a one-sided charity case."

"Well, Faris and I *are* sacrificing a lot to help you."

Joanne drew her eyebrows together. "You and *Faris*? What does your husband have to do with anything?"

"Oh my God. You can't be serious, Joanne. Did you think I'd just invite some girl over to spend hours alone with our daughter and not ask his permission?"

"His *permission*?" Joanne looked at her friend, hands gripping the steering wheel. "You mean letting my daughter come over requires some major family deliberation?"

"Well, actually, it does."

Speechless, Joanne stared at Basma. It was only the sound of a beeping horn that prompted Joanne to blink and shake her head. She lifted her foot from the brake and rested it on the gas pedal, guiding the car past the green light.

"In an Islamic household," Basma said, her voice authoritative despite the soft tone. "that's how it should be."

"In an *Islamic* household?" Joanne contorted her face. "So what does that make *my* household?"

"Joanne, don't be unreasonable. I just want you to know it's not personal."

"But it is personal, Basma. It's very personal."

Joanne squinted her eyes as she glanced at her friend. "Think about it. Do you have to get permission every time Maryam's *cousins* want to drop by?"

"They're family, Joanne. That's different. We have to keep ti—"

"In *Islam*," Joanne said, her emphasis on the word intentionally sarcastic, "cousins aren't family. Otherwise, how did you and Faris get married?"

"Wh…" Basma's eyes widened, but Joanne could tell Basma didn't know what to say.

"And isn't it true," Joanne said, "your husband can forbid *family* from visiting if he thinks they'll cause harm?"

"Well…yes…but—"

"But nothing, Basma. So it's personal. Period. There's no need to lie about it." Joanne's nose flared. She shook her head. "And Islam forbids lying last time I checked."

Basma sighed, and Joanne sensed her friend wasn't in the mood to argue.

Joanne felt a tinge of guilt pinching her, but she found it difficult to let go of her offense. How could Basma think she was corrupt?

Joanne huffed. Was this what her life would forever be as a Muslim? Other Muslims holding her at arm's length? Admiring because she's American, but distrusting for the same reason?

Shaking her head, Joanne propped her left elbow on the seal of the window next to her as her right hand steered the car. Oh how she'd believed all that universal brotherhood rhetoric when she first accepted Islam. But now…what was left for her? Not even the marriage she'd thrown her heart into sustaining. She now lived an ocean apart from her youngest children. The two boys she loved more than life itself were with their father in Saudi Arabia.

Joanne was tired of hearing how Islam is perfect and Muslims are imperfect or how she shouldn't judge Islam by the actions of Muslims.

"Oh please," an American convert had said once, rolling her eyes. *"That's just what they say so they can keep living culture and ignoring Islam."*

At the time, Joanne had been infuriated. She was personally offended because she was married into one of the very cultures the woman was criticizing. "I swear to God these Black people are impossible," Joanne had said to Riaz later that day. "People bend over backwards to treat them equal, but it's never enough." Riaz had laughed in agreement as she continued venting. "They're a bunch of ungrateful leeches if you ask me. Always got their hands out, but then they complain that even the people who *help* them are racist!"

These were the words that hung in Joanne's mind as she pulled the car to a stop in front of the Muslim high school where the girls were finishing a placement exam.

Joanne felt the beginning of a headache. She was beginning to see the world with the very eyes she'd scorned for so long.

"Oh, sweetheart, don't blame yourself," Riaz had said when he'd sat her down to explain his reasons for divorce. *"It's not your fault. It's just that this has been really hard for my family."*

What the—? Joanne had thought at the time. Was he kidding? You're just going to throw away a marriage of fifteen years because your wife doesn't "fit in" the family? *You knew I couldn't speak Urdu or cook biryani when you married me!*

"Joanne," Basma's soft voice drifted to Joanne as if from a distance, "are you okay?"

Joanne's heart beat had slowed to a normal rate, but the tightening in her chest had not loosened.

It's not personal, Joanne.

Such simple, sincere words Basma had spoken. Yet they were eerily similar to the ones Riaz had used to break apart an entire family.

Yes, I know it's not personal, Basma, Joanne thought as she turned the keys to shut off the engine. *My problem is one I can't control.*

The keys jingled as she pulled them out the ignition.

I exist.

Read full story in the novel *The Friendship Promise* at uzauthor.com

Black Women Don't Need To Cover?

a short story

Faith and Grace, American expats living in Saudi Arabia, discuss culture shock at the way Arabs view black women.

~

UMM ZAKIYYAH

"Why isn't the Qur'an and Sunnah sufficient for us?" Faith said, her hands trembling behind her head as she unfastened her *niqaab*. She tossed the face veil to a nearby table and collapsed into the softness of the couch, the cloth of her *khimaar* loosening itself from where it framed the brown of her face.

Grace smiled as she closed the door to her villa and joined her friend on the couch. Grace reached forward and poured coffee into a small glass cup and handed it to her friend. "Still in culture shock after five years?"

Faith groaned and rolled her eyes as she accepted the coffee, but she held the glass in her hand without drinking it. "You won't believe what my Saudi friend just told me."

Grace sighed, but her expression remained pleasant. "What now?"

"That the *niqaab* isn't obligatory for black women."

Grace huffed. "I'm not surprised. I was told I have to cover my face because I'm white." She shook her head then added, "*And* my eyes because they're blue."

"Where do these people learn their religion?" Faith shook her head. "I thought I was coming to a country where I'd feel better as a Muslim, not worse." Grace laughed. "Didn't we all?"

"I had to pull my children out of Qur'an school," Faith said. "Can you believe that?"

Grace's eyes widened. "Why?"

"Because the teacher's constantly making anti-American remarks, and the students are always calling my children racist names." Faith drew in a deep breath and exhaled. "My daughter won't even look in the mirror anymore. She thinks she's ugly."

Grace sighed thoughtfully. "My children are facing the same thing."

Faith's eyes widened. "Are you serious? I thought white people had it easier here."

"I meant the anti-American part," Grace said. "I've been Muslim for fifteen years, and I'm still treated like I don't know anything about Islam."

Faith's gaze grew distant, and she sipped her coffee in silence while Grace served herself a cup.

"You know what bothers me most about that 'black women don't have to cover' remark?" Faith said, her tone thoughtful.

Grace took a sip of coffee. "What's that?"

"Here, they believe covering the face is obligatory."

Grace sighed and nodded. "That bothered me for a while too. But you have to admit, they do have a point. Even some Muslim scholars say that."

"That's not what I mean," Faith said. "I completely understand the Islamic reasons for the difference of opinion. And to be honest, I feel most comfortable in *niqaab*, even in America."

"Then what's bothering you?"

"Think about it, Grace," Faith said, setting down her coffee cup and turning herself toward her friend. "They say that covering the face *is* hijab."

"Yeah, of course," Grace said. "That's what they mean when they say wearing *niqaab* is obligatory."

Faith laughed. "That's exactly my point. Don't you see how messed up this is?"

Grace creased her forehead and shook her head. "I'm not following you."

"Think about it," Faith said. "Allah tells the believing women to wear hijab."

"Okay…"

"And in Saudi Arabia, they say hijab means covering the face."

Grace nodded. "Yeah."

"But then they say a certain group of believing women can ignore what Allah says."

Grace's eyes widened in understanding. "Oh my God. I never thought about it like that."

"And what reason do they give?" Faith asked rhetorically.

Grace shook her head knowingly, a smile forming on her face.

"That these women are so ugly," Faith said, answering her own question, "that even Allah's commands don't apply to them."

"Wow…" Grace said, shaking her head in disbelief.

Grace narrowed her eyes thoughtfully. "But maybe your friend doesn't believe it's obligatory."

"But, Grace," Faith said, humor in her tone, "even if she doesn't, what right does she have to declare a group of Allah's creation ugly, and then have Islamic opinions based on it?" She shook her head. "I swear, even when I was a disbeliever in America, I never heard something like that."

Grace grunted laughter. "You know, that's what gets me so upset when they tell me I have to cover my face because I'm white. It's like these Arab men sit around and decide which women are a *fitnah* for them, and my life has to revolve around what they decide." She laughed again. "And they have the nerve to say this is from Islam."

Faith sighed. "You know what's so sad?"

Grace looked at her friend.

"Nobody's speaking out against this stuff," Faith said.

"I think people are," Grace said. "When I travel to America, Saudi Arabia's all people talk about when they speak about women's issues in the Middle East."

"I mean *here*," Faith said. "Who's talking about it here?"

Grace nodded. "I see what you mean."

"Okay," Faith said, "to a certain extent, I can excuse Saudis for being silent because, honestly, I don't think they know what racism is."

Grace laughed. "Faith, come on. They know what racism is. My husband and I talk about this problem all the time."

"But, Grace, your husband grew up in America. He's Saudi by passport, not culture."

Grace nodded. "Yeah, but a lot of Saudis are starting to realize there's a big problem here with how they treat non-Saudis."

"I don't think so," Faith said. "They don't even pay people based on qualifications. It's based on nationality."

"That doesn't mean they don't know it's wrong."

"Well, I guess you have more faith in them than I do."

"Saudis aren't all the same, Faith," Grace said. "My husband's family is really upset about what's happening here. But there's not much they can do. They're almost as powerless as we are."

Faith sighed. "Maybe you're right."

The friends were silent for some time.

"But can't they just leave Islam out of it?" Faith said, her tone reflective. "It's really dangerous to mix racism and Islam."

"I think the problem is mixing human opinion with Islam," Grace said. "And unfortunately, Saudi Arabia's not the only country that does this. It's a problem all over the world."

"But why?" Faith said, her eyes narrowed in frustration. "We can't just make up rules from our minds." She sighed and shook her head. "When is this going to stop?"

Grace smiled as she met her friend's gaze. "When the Qur'an and Sunnah is sufficient for us."

The
Day Jessica
Left Islam

a short story

Jessica, an American convert to Islam, attends a dinner party, and the hostess's underhanded scheme and troublesome comments spur Jessica's decision to give up being Muslim.

~

UMM
ZAKIYYAH

"Sit."

Jessica turned from where she was parting the heavily brocaded curtains to peer outside into the darkness. She found a large woman with deep olive skin gesturing toward a crushed velvet cushion on a chair in the dining room. The woman's gold embroidered traditional dress that was wrapped about her made Jessica wish she could be in the comfort of her own apartment right then. She had missed *American Idol* to come tonight, she thought sadly. It was hard to believe that just a year before she had auditioned to be on the show. But she imagined she would have to give up dancing for good now...

"Sit," the woman said again, "We will have tea."

It was then that Jessica remembered the woman from earlier. The woman's accent had slightly distorted the intonations of the brief English outbursts she had used to command the servers who couldn't seem to set up or clear out fast enough for the woman's tastes.

"Useless," Jessica remembered hearing the woman mutter in a low voice after a server scurried from the room swaying under the weight of the stack of glass plates with half-eaten food on them. Then the woman began chatting in a language that Jessica did not recognize or understand.

"Thank you," Jessica murmured as made her way to the table. But she didn't feel thankful. She felt suffocated and overwhelmed. The house smelled of scented burning wood and she wondered if it would be rude to open a window.

"Islam means peace," a burly imām with a large beard had told her two months before, when she still hadn't gotten up the nerve to become Muslim though she knew it was the right thing to do. "When you say the *shahādah*, all your sins are wiped away. And you feel new."

But Jessica didn't feel new. She didn't even feel peace. She just felt...lonely, incredibly lonely. How would she tell her parents? They would kill her...

"You enjoy yourself tonight, no?" the woman asked after she and Jessica seated themselves across from each other at the long polished oak wood table. The woman was arranging a silver tea set as she spoke.

"Sorry about my mom," a girl had leaned down to whisper to Jessica after most of the guests had gone home. Jessica's gaze followed the teenager who was tucking a soiled tablecloth under one arm, but the girl kept moving and didn't wait for a reply.

At the moment, the apology had confused Jessica, but Jessica's now heightened discomfort inspired the vague feeling that she was about to have tea with the girl's mother, whom Jessica assumed owned the large home where the party had been held.

"I'm sorry about staying here so long," Jessica said, glancing at the window she had been looking out earlier. "It's just that they told me—"

"Nonsense," the woman said with a wave of her hand as she reached for the teapot and poured hot water into a small china glass, then reached across the table to set it in front of Jessica. "You are not an imposition."

Jessica quickly tore open a package of artificial sweetener and emptied the powder into her hot water, stirring it vigorously with the small silver tea spoon. She clumsily brought the small cup to her lips in an effort to quiet the laughter she felt erupting at the back of her throat. It was incredibly rude to mock how a person spoke. Maybe it was the stress of the night getting to her, but she should know better, even if she had been Muslim for only three weeks.

But the sound of the woman's accent mixed with the "perfect English" was annoying, a feeling that had, even as a child, often inspired laughter in Jessica. She would have to keep her composure until Damon arrived to take her home. Then they could laugh about it together in the car…

"You are married, no?"

Jessica looked up suddenly from behind the teacup that was still at her lips, her eyes widened. She gulped the liquid and shuddered at the stinging heat in her throat. She coughed to avoid the piercing gaze of the woman with dark eyes and a determined expression that made Jessica squirm in her seat as she set her cup down.

"No, I, uh—" Jessica didn't know how to respond. She was only 19 years old and in the spring term of her second year in undergrad. Marriage had never crossed her mind. The only ring she wore right then was on the middle finger of her right hand, and was a simple sterling silver band she'd bought at Claire's when she was in high school. So she had no idea what made this imposing woman ask the question.

Jessica stole a glance at her watch and groaned inwardly as she realized that it would be at least another forty minutes before her friend would arrive. The women at the masjid had said the party would end around 10:30 or 11:00, and Jessica had imagined she was being overly polite when she'd asked Damon to come at 10:00. She was mortified when she saw the final guests drifting out at 9:00.

"I can't," Damon's voice had crackled through her cell phone after she slipped to a corner of the living room to phone him and ask if he could come earlier. "I have to take the Bar again tomorrow, Jessie. You know that, and I need the extra time to study."

"So he is your *boy*friend?" the woman's voice rose as her heavy hands daintily placed her small teacup on its saucer. The woman was looking directly at Jessica, blinking repeatedly. The woman's polite expression only thinly veiled the disapproval on her middle-aged face.

Jessica's stomach churned. She dropped her gaze to the cup she now cradled in her hands. She sensed the woman's emphasis on the word "boy" had nothing to do with English being a second language.

"Next thing they'll tell you is you can't talk to me," Damon had told her, grunting, when she first expressed to him her interest in becoming Muslim.

"You're just being cynical," she'd said. He had laughed then, a laugh of pity. *"You'll see,"* he had said quietly, seeming to be talking more to himself than her.

"No, no, no," Jessica said, shaking her head, a smile now toying at the sides of her mouth as she tried to appear composed before the woman. She felt her cheeks go warm as she realized her reply suggested she was hiding something shameful.

"Then you are just roaming about here and there with a strange man?"

There was an awkward pause, and the sound of a car approaching outside sent Jessica's heart racing in embarrassment and hope. Then the sound faded.

"No, of course not..." Jessica said, realizing she couldn't recall the woman's name. There had been so many to keep up with, and none of them had been in English. Would she have to change her name too? O Lord, her mother would have a fit. "...I've known him since we were kids."

"Hmph." The woman poured more water into Jessica's cup and the woman's eyes concentrated on this task briefly before looking at Jessica again. "He is Muslim, then, of course?"

It was an accusation, not a question. But Jessica decided that the woman had a right to disapprove, even if she didn't have a right to pry. Jessica was still learning all the rules in Islam, and though she really wanted to learn, she was scared she'd learn one more thing she'd have to give up. Hadn't it been enough to give up professional dancing? O God! That had been her *life*. Would she have to give up Damon too?

Jessica's heart dropped at the thought, and she averted her gaze. "No, he's um...."

The sudden shrilling of a phone made Jessica start. She immediately looked toward her own purse, but when the phone rang again, Jessica realized it was coming from across the room.

The woman stood quickly and walked noisily toward the source of the sound.

"Ah, so he has now arrived," the woman said seconds later in her accented too-perfect English. "Jessica and I have been waiting anxiously for him to come." A pause. "Oh, nonsense. We are happy to meet him."

Jessica furrowed her brow. How had Damon gotten the house number? She reached for her purse and pulled the strap over her shoulder, relieved despite her confusion. She doubted she could last another minute here...

The woman's wide smile revealed slightly yellowing teeth as she approached Jessica after hanging up the phone. "Sit, sit, sit," the woman said flapping her hands like a child. "My son is here now. You will meet him. He is a doctor, you see. Very, very busy. So, so busy. You see, he is doing his residency at Johns Hopkins. You know Johns Hopkins, no? The best, the best."

"But—" Jessica's eyes grew large. "I, why...your son? But..."

"Nonsense," the woman cut her off. "You will meet him. You will talk. And then—" The woman caught herself, as if realizing just then that her words may offend Jessica in some way. The woman exhaled loudly instead, a smile returning to her face a moment later. "—Well, then, after that, we shall see. We shall see."

Jessica stood with her mouth gaping open.

"Sit, darling, sit. And oh," the woman said, quickly turning to Jessica as if remembering something just then. "You can remove that, that..." The woman pointed to Jessica's head. "...cloth. At moments like these, there's no need for all these restrictions. You are American, so you understand, no?"

Instinctively, Jessica's hand went protectively to the soft blue *khimaar* she had worn all evening. She didn't wear the cloth to school or in public, but still…

"I ain't feeling it," Damon had said as she checked herself in the sun visor mirror after wrapping it around her before he dropped her off. *"But it suits you, I suppose."*

"Oh, hijab!" a young woman had squealed in excitement when Jessica had come through the door. *"Quick, quick! Get a camera. Ooooh, māshā'Allāh, and it brings out her eyes doesn't it? Congratulations, Jessica! You're a better Muslim than we are!"*

"How did it go?" Damon asked as Jessica climbed clumsily into the car and threw her head back in exhaustion, the blue *khimaar* now crumpled and tucked into a pocket of her jacket. But of course Damon wouldn't notice the difference. He'd probably forgotten she'd had it on in the first place.

With her head still leaning on the back of her seat, she turned to him and noticed the exhaustion in his eyes. He was barely awake enough to drive. She sighed knowing it was useless to respond honestly, but she felt tears stinging her eyes.

"Let us talk frankly, Jessica," the woman had said when her not-so-excited son had come into the room still wearing his doctor's coat. He had looked at Jessica sideways, apologizing in that glance. *Sorry about my mom*, he seemed to say, as his sister had earlier. But he kept his lips locked into a thin line, his exhaustion as palpable as Damon's was right then.

"You are not in a relationship with this Black man you are roaming about with, no? He is only a driver, no?" She then turned to her son, eagerness and apology in her tone.

Jessica had been too shocked to speak…

"See, Abdullah, it is only a rumor, a vicious rumor. You know how ladies are, tongues wagging, no sense, no sense. It is nothing, nothing at all. He is an 'abeed, nothing more, like our driver back home. Uff! No sensible woman would marry a useless servant. These Americans are more up to date than we are, son."

The woman had then turned to Jessica. *"Let us talk frankly, dear. You are like my daughter, Wallah. You Americans are hospitable to the Blacks here, are you not? Muslims at heart, you are, wallah! So kind, so kind. And we are too in our countries. But he cannot be your friend, dear. Impossible. Too many people will judge us..."*

Us. That's the word that had made Jessica's parted lips snap shut for the rest of the evening...

"So it went well?" Damon asked reaching for the paper cup of coffee from the cup holder between them. He took a sip, set the cup back in its place, then brought his free hand to his mouth to stifle a yawn. The silence of the night was comforting, and only the sounds of passing cars whizzing by could be heard.

"Yes, it went well," Jessica said dryly. She looked out the window beside her into the darkness. The passing trees and familiar scenery made a lump develop in her throat. She missed her parents right then. She wanted to fly home just to give them a hug, crying in their arms. *I'm so sorry, Mom and Dad. So sorry. You won't lose me again. I don't know if I could ever be Christian again, but I learned one thing tonight. Just one thing, and by God! I love you for it. You are not hypocrites. You are not hypocrites...*

"That's good, that's good..." Damon muttered. A few seconds passed before he sighed and turned to her briefly.

"Jessie, I'm sorry about not supporting you and all. It's just that..."

Jessica drew in a deep breath and exhaled, her chin quivering as her thoughts finished his sentence. *I already know, Damon. I already know. ...It's just that you knew better than me.*

From the Diary of an Extremist

a short story

An American college student converts to Islam and makes the decision to wear all black and cover her face. But she faces opposition from where she least expects—from fellow Muslims themselves.

~

UMM ZAKIYYAH

"Go back to your country! We don't want you here!"

The words still echoed in my mind as I crossed through the carpeted lobby of the Student Union building. Students sat in huddles on the floor, others sitting lazily on the arms of couches occasionally laughing at something someone said. When I walked by, the voices quieted suddenly. Like needles pricking me all over, I felt their eyes following me.

But no one said anything.

I held my breath until I rounded the corner where there was a staircase leading to the second level. I didn't like taking the elevator. It was too uncomfortable. I never knew who'd end up riding the short ascension with me. Besides, thirty steps never killed anyone.

At least I hadn't heard of it if it had.

When I pulled open the heavy door, I heard a burst of laughter from the lobby that was so distinct from the earlier banter that I knew that I had, again, been the butt of a joke.

I sighed, letting my footfalls on the steps distract me from the pounding in my chest. My face burned and I wondered how long I could hold up. I had been wearing *niqaab* for eight months, but I was still adjusting to life in the face veil.

No one told me it'd be like this.

Yes, Neveen had warned me that people wouldn't like it, but I mean, this? Oh my God. Do these people have a life? All I do is dress how I want—which is what I thought my American nationality gave me right to—and I don't have a day of peace in my life. If it wasn't one thing, it was another.

"Are you a terrorist?" a woman had asked me at the mall. When I turned around all prepared with my sarcastic reply, I saw her eyes widened and her jaw dropped in a stupor, as if she really, I mean *really*, expected an answer.

If I hadn't been so irritated, I would have laughed. The first response that came to my mind was, *Well, if you really thought I was a terrorist, would you feel comfortable coming up and asking me?*

But I just smiled—not that she'd benefit from that gesture since my *niqaab* concealed my face—and said politely, "No, ma'am. I'm a Muslim." I paused until her mouth opened wider as she got over the fact that I could actually speak perfect English, no doubt. "And you should be Muslim too."

At that, I had walked away, my heart pounding in my chest, seething at the ignorance—and audacity—of people.

Presently, my heart softened as I saw the MSA room ahead of me. It looked so official, the nameplate on the door: "Muslim Student Association."

I let out a breath of relief as I pulled open the door. The soft sound of Qur'an wafted from the speakers in the corner of the room, and tears welled in my eyes at the beautiful recitation of *Surah Ar-Rahmaan*—the Qur'anic chapter entitled "The Most Gracious."

The room smelled of sweet incense and I breathed in the scent of home. I took a seat at the table and glanced around. There was no sign of Amira—the MSA vice president. I checked my watch. It was 11:31. I was only a minute late. Hopefully, she hadn't forgotten about me.

I flipped up my face veil before removing my notebook from my bag and opening it to review my notes in preparation for the meeting. My heartbeat had slowed to a comfortable rhythm, but for some reason I was a bit nervous. The last time I'd met with the MSA officially was the year before, when I was vice president myself. At the time, Amira had been the secretary, and we met at least twice a week to brainstorm ideas for the organization.

I looked over my list of concerns and suggestions:
- Movie Night (concern)
- Potluck Night, one for men, one for women (suggestion)
- Music during social events (concern)

- Nasheeds played instead (suggestion)

I frowned. It was much shorter than my original list. But I trusted Neveen more than myself, so I had taken her advice and chose brevity over venting. It was hard not to vent though. Sometimes I felt as if my *jilbaab* and *niqaab* were not only a barrier between me and non-Muslims, but also a barrier between me and other Muslims. It just didn't seem fair. I had expected to be voted out of my vice president position, but I hadn't expected to feel like an outsider in the MSA itself. This, Neveen hadn't warned me about.

"Don't expect too much," she had told me earlier that morning. "People aren't really open to these types of changes."

"I think they'll be open," I told her. I had always been somewhat of an optimist. "Besides, if anyone can convince them, I can. Amira and I were best friends. She's the one who—"

"I know, Latifah. I just don't want you to get your hopes up. I know Amira's really sweet, but you have to realize that you've changed and—"

"I haven't changed," I said, a bit offended. "I'm the same person. All I did was put on a *jilbaab* and *niqaab*."

"But that's not how they see it. To them, you're a…" She averted her gaze and looked out the window momentarily as she searched for the word.

"A what?"

Sighing, she met my gaze. "Extremist."

I felt my face grow hot in anger. "An extremist?" I narrowed my eyes. "Neveen, how could you even think something like that? These people are like family to me. Yes, we have our disagreements, but I love Amira like a sister. She's the one who taught me about Islam. And the MSA is the closest thing I have to a family. I don't care what differences we have, I'll always love them for giving me a home when my parents turned their backs on me after I became Muslim."

My eyes had begun to water as I reflected on how much these people meant to me. "They're all I have," I told Neveen, "and whatever they say or do, I'll stick by them because they're my brothers and sisters in Islam. We all make mistakes. I don't think it's fair to accuse them of something like that."

She shrugged. "You're right. I'm sorry. Maybe I'm overreacting."

"Yes, you are," I said, still a bit angry about her extremist comment. "Now tell me what you think I should say at the meeting."

Presently, the door to the MSA room opened and Amira entered. She smiled and walked over to me, extending her hand as she greeted me. "*As-salaamu 'alaikum*. I'm sorry I'm late. My meeting with Rahim went longer than I expected."

"Oh, I'm sorry. I didn't know you had another meeting."

Without responding, she took a seat across from me and set down the clipboard she was holding. I was only half aware of the document and fifty-dollar bill attached to the clipboard.

"Okay," she said, letting out a sigh. "Let's just get started. I don't want to take too much of your time. First, I'll let you explain why you—"

"Let me turn off the Qur'an first," I said, getting up and walking over to the CD player and pressing the off button. When I returned to my seat, I saw that Amira looked a bit agitated, but I didn't know why.

"Like I said," she began again. "I'll let you start first, then I'll tell you what conclusions we've come to."

I didn't understand her last comment, seeing as though I had called the meeting and hadn't yet told her my concerns. How then could she and Rahim have come to any conclusions?

Not wanting to get distracted, I told her my concerns, all the while hearing Neveen in my head telling me to be calm, diplomatic, and understanding of their point of view.

When I finished, I exhaled, realizing just then how nervous I was.

"Okay, Latifah. Let me just be honest with you." Amira leaned forward on her elbows with her hands clasped. "We were very upset that you didn't tell us you were coming to movie night a couple of weeks ago. I mean, you've never come before, and then all of a sudden, you show up? You could've called to tell Rahim, or me at least."

I creased my forehead in confusion. "Tell you? But…"

"Honestly," Amira said, "I feel like all you do is come to things to sabotage them. You never have anything good to say. And you made everyone feel really uncomfortable that night."

She narrowed her eyes, hurt. "Did you even realize that we had invited the dean to that event?"

I felt myself growing defensive. "But I didn't even say anything there. I just sat in the back and watched the movie."

"That's the point, Latifah. You didn't say anything. You just sat back and watched. And everyone else interacted, talked, laughed, and tried to enjoy themselves." She shook her head. "I thought you didn't watch movies anymore."

I didn't know what to say. "I don't," I said. "It's just that it was a Black History Month program, and the movie…" I lost my train of thought for a second.

"*Something the Lord Made*," she said in a flat tone, staring at me unblinking.

"Yeah, I've seen it before, and I knew it was clean, so I thought—"

"You thought. What about what we thought? How do you think it feels to have the dean sitting there with his wife enjoying the evening, and then walks in some, some…" She wrinkled her nose as she searched for the right word.

"…some terrorist for all they know. I mean, you don't even have the decency to wear something presentable. It's always the same thing, that ugly black sheet. God, Latifah, last year you had so much style. You wore colors, *bright* colors." Her nose flared. "And now," she contorted her face as she gestured a hand toward me, "*this*."

I was so stunned at her words that I was only vaguely aware of the tears gathering in Amira's eyes.

"I don't know what is going on with you," she said, "but you can't keep this up. I'm scared for you."

"But…" I stammered, feeling my face go hot and tears sting my eyes. "What does this have to do with anything? We've always hosted events about diversity. We even have meetings on ways to make non-practicing Muslims feel welcome. I don't understand what—"

"Of course you don't understand, Latifah. You've been brainwashed. And I hope to God that you wake up soon."

"Brainwashed?"

"Yes. Wearing that stupid mask on your face, looking like a ninja. And then all of a sudden, music is *haraam*, movies are *haraam*, and talking to men is *haraam*. I really don't—"

"What? I can't believe what you're saying, Amira. All I suggested is that we try to be more sensitive to other people and more mindful of intermingling when we—"

"There you go again. *Intermingling*." She shook her head.

"I have things to do," she said before I could respond, "so let me just get to the point."

I felt as if my face was on fire. I didn't know what to say. This was surreal. She couldn't be serious. I mean, even if she listened to music and watched R-rated movies herself, certainly she realized that there were hundreds of other Muslims who didn't. And my *jilbaab* was a problem now? Oh my God. I didn't know what to say. All I was doing was obeying what Allah said in the Qur'an and dressing as the female companions of the Prophet, peace be upon him, had dressed. Even if Amira didn't want to dress as they had, what was so wrong with my doing it?

"Here."

I looked up to find Amira standing, the clipboard under one arm and the fifty-dollar bill in her other hand outstretched toward me.

I gathered my eyebrows. "What's this for?"

"You."

I still didn't get it.

"It's a refund for your MSA dues."

"Wh-wh...?"

"Yes, Latifah, a refund. You heard me right. I already spoke to the dean of the school, and he agreed that this is the only way to solve the problem. It's already official. We've revoked your membership."

I was speechless as I stared at her.

When I didn't accept the bill, she let it drop to the table.

"When you get past this crazy phase," she said, "I'm here. It's just that right now, we can't risk having extremists in the MSA. It's bad for *da'wah*. And, honestly, it's bad for us."

At that, she walked away, opened the door, and let it close behind her; and I was left in the silence of the room. But now, I didn't even have the Qur'an to comfort me.

Right then, in my mind there was the faint echo of the women's words from earlier that day, and at that moment, they took on an entirely new meaning. *"Go back to your country! We don't want you here!"*

The
Invitation

a short story

Faith and Paula are childhood friends who accept Islam just as Faith's relationship with her boyfriend, John, becomes serious…and just as Paula comes out as gay. With their newfound Muslim identity, must Faith sacrifice John, and Paula her sexuality?

~

UMM
ZAKIYYAH

PART ONE

I hugged my knees and concentrated my attention on the parking lot beyond my third-floor apartment window. It was all I could do to steady my trembling and think of something besides the torn envelope and embossed card next to me on the crumpled sheet of my bed.

I was upset. I knew that much. But there was something deeper knifing at my heart.

Your attendance is requested at the wedding celebration of...

I gritted my teeth until my jaws hurt.

Betrayal. The feeling sliced through me so suddenly that for a moment I stopped shaking.

Fourteen Years Before

Life as I knew it ended a week after my ninth birthday. It was late May, right when a month of school felt like a year, and the days dragged on until the desire for summer drove everyone, even the teachers, to a mixture of madness and dejection. Schoolwork was no longer displayed on classroom walls. Decorations were slowly and surreptitiously removed from bulletin boards, and the hall monitors turned a blind eye to students lingering in the corridors without a pass. And even failing students held a flicker of optimism because teachers no longer had the energy or concern to hold students back.

Later, I'd find myself wondering if my life would have turned out differently had my mother's energy or concern for my future mirrored the pity teachers had for hopeless students...

I came home aggravated as usual. I was tired of the rushed homework assignments that I had to cram into my schedule every night because yet another teacher wanted to finish the book before the year ended.

"Faith! Is that you?"

I threw my backpack on the tiled floor of the foyer and groaned as I shut the front door. Who else would it be? "Yeah, Mom!" I yelled back.

"Come here, sweetie."

I groaned. I already knew something was wrong because my mother never called me "sweetie" unless there was bad news or she wanted me to do something I loathed, like clean the bathroom.

"Mo-om," I whined before I even dragged myself into the den, where I was certain she was sitting in front of some stupid soap opera.

I was surprised to find her on the couch in front of a darkened television screen. She forced a smile when I entered, and I saw the thinly veiled sadness on her face. I kept my arms folded, and my face twisted only because it didn't make sense to change my stance or soften my pout. But I sensed my mom was trying to cheer me up to lighten the blow, and that's when a sick feeling came over me and I knew something was wrong. As awkward as it sounds, this was the first moment I actually saw my mother, I mean really saw her.

In retrospect, I should have known. I know I was only nine, but really, let's be frank here. My mom was a fiery redhead with blue eyes, and my dad, who shared my mom's eye color, was so blond that he was often mistaken for an albino. And they both shared that pale, colorless complexion that the sun blotched instead of tanned, not to mention their straight, limp hair that wouldn't curl even when it grew long. I, on the other hand, had dark brown eyes, kinky black hair that only braids and thick ponytail holders could keep in place. And my skin looked like latte with a generous portion of milk.

Yet stupidly, I'd thought nothing of how my playmate and neighbor, Paula, was often mistaken for my parents' daughter and I her best friend, instead of the other way around. It was something we'd laugh about. But in that moment before my mother spoke aloud what I should have known all along, I saw my parents for who they were: two middle-aged, White people who had everything they could want in life, except the hope of ever having a child of their own...

Five Years Before

"I'm so happy for you!" Paula squealed as she drew me into a brief hug as I stepped into the foyer of her parents' home. I wore a smug grin as I shrugged off my coat and stepped out of my muddy boots. I usually didn't bother taking off my shoes when I visited, but I didn't want to soil the plush carpet.

"But are you sure?" Paula said, drawing her eyebrows together as she regarded me.

I looped my arm through hers as we walked toward the stairs leading to her bedroom. "Mm hm," I said, giddy as a kid who'd won a trip to Disney World. "Positive."

"Oh my God," she said as she hurried up the stairs, almost dragging me beside her. "You have to tell me everything! How are they?"

I laughed as she ushered me into her room and closed the door. "I don't know yet..." A tightness formed in my throat, and a twinge of sadness weakened me. What if my birth parents didn't want to meet me? Just because I was eighteen now and had a right to find them without my adopted parents knowing didn't mean my birth parents would *want* me to find them. But I had found them. Or at least the agency I'd paid with the money from my part-time job at the mall had found them. Now it was just a matter of waiting to see if they wanted to be found.

"But John is really supportive," I offered, a smile plastered on my face as I sat down on the edge of her bed.

"That's good." Paula's tone was distracted as she sat beside me, one leg folded between us. I hated the way she acted whenever I mentioned my boyfriend. He was the first boy I met that I really connected with, and although I'd only known him for a few months, I really felt like he was "the one." I'd never felt like that with anyone else. Why couldn't she be happy for me? She knew how much anxiety I usually felt around guys. That's why I was still a virgin while most of my classmates debated whether or not "respectable girls" could have one-night stands.

Paula herself would often tease me about being so "compulsive" about intimacy with the opposite sex. She went through boyfriends like most girls went through lipstick. In a way, I envied her. I wanted to feel that freedom with myself and my body, but I just couldn't. Paula had all these radical ideas about feminism and women opposing patriarchal oppression, especially with regards to the female body, and to be honest, it sounded really convincing. But it just wasn't me. I wasn't sure if I was backwards or just old-fashioned. But if I gave myself to someone, it would have to be someone special, someone I wanted to spend the rest of my life with. And I was beginning to feel like John was that person...

"I'm sorry, Faith," Paula said with a sigh. "I'm really happy for you and John. It's just..." Her voice trailed as her eyes stared at something beyond my head. "...I wish I could find someone too."

Finding Islam

Paula and I met Sommer during a community service summer internship hosted by an Ivy League university for graduating seniors. During introductions when we were asked to say something we loved about ourselves, Sommer humorously said, "I'm a spunky, Arab-Pakistani who loves rock music, and I don't give a damn what anyone else thinks."

Ironically, the first time Sommer spoke to me and Paula directly was in response to a sarcastic remark she'd overhead Paula make about her hijab.

"You judge women without even letting them speak for themselves," Sommer retorted, rolling her eyes. "And you call yourself a feminist?"

Even I had to admit she had a point. But of course, Paula couldn't let Sommer have the last word, so they went at it all through lunch break. They even continued their argument that evening in the dormitory hallway until some girls told them to shut up. But even then neither would back down, so I reluctantly told them to at least get out the hallway. And of course that meant they would argue in the dorm room that I was sharing with Paula for those eight weeks. As their voices rose to deafening levels right there in my room, I threw myself into bed and put a pillow over my head to drown out their voices, hoping to at one point, miraculously, fall asleep.

"No it's not. No it's not," I said, my voice picking up pitch as the feeling of desperation overtook me. *"No it's not!"* My eyes shot open, and beneath my comforter, my heart pounded with the same frustrated conviction that it had in the dream. I glanced around the room, and it took several seconds before I realized where I was. I sat up, drained, as if the heated exchange had been real.

The lingering sensation of my protest made me feel sick and hopeful at once, but I didn't understand this feeling.

How could I? I had no idea what I was even arguing about in the dream, or with whom. All I could remember was seeing a faded red-heart tattoo on some girl's lower back and feeling so close and distant from myself at once. I knew I was yelling at the tattooed girl, but I don't know what about. But the more I yelled, the farther she was out of my reach, and the closer to myself I felt. There were black snakes and lizards coming toward the girl, but she didn't see them because she was so happy and content with whatever she was telling me. "No it's not," I kept saying in response. "No it's not!" Right before I woke up, I was in a green pasture alone, far from the girl, but I was still yelling even though I was losing my voice and I knew the tattooed girl could no longer hear me.

In that moment, as I sat up in the stillness of late night, I realized that the tattooed girl was most likely me and that the dream was some sort of sign. Suddenly, I wanted to talk to John. He had always been more spiritual than I was, and I wondered if he would know what the dream meant.

I glanced around in the darkness of the dorm room and saw that Paula was sleeping soundly under her covers. I vaguely recalled Paula and Sommer arguing before I fell asleep, and I wondered when the argument ended and when Sommer had finally gone back to her own room. I remembered how upset I was that they would argue like that when I wanted to sleep. I sighed at the thought. But I decided against calling John until morning.

I don't know why, but at breakfast, I loosely mentioned the dream to Paula but only the part about yelling out in the green pasture and feeling close and distant from myself and my hunch that it was some sort of spiritual sign. "Maybe Sommer might know what it means," she casually suggested before shoving a forkful of scrambled eggs into her mouth.

Before I could protest or get over the fact that she imagined that Sommer would even speak to her, Paula got up and found Sommer and asked her to come sit with us. To my surprise, Sommer agreed, and casually said, "What's up?" as she slid into the space next to Paula and across from me. I opened my mouth to tell her it's nothing, but Paula shut me up by talking over me and recounting what I'd told her of the dream.

"It means you're going to find the truth," Sommer said simply, her dark eyes serious as she met my gaze. She either didn't notice my shocked expression or was unfazed by it. "And after you find it," she said, glancing briefly at her plate as she sliced into her pancake with the side of her fork, "you're going to be tempted by yourself or someone you love to give up your faith, but you won't *insha'Allah*." She quickly added, "God-willing, I mean."

"But…" I stammered. I didn't know what to say. "How do you know? Are you psychic or something?"

Sommer laughed and reached up to smooth down her white hijab. "True dreams are gifts from God. You either understand the signs He gives, or you don't. Being psychic has nothing to do with it."

"But how do you know what the signs mean?"

"I don't," Sommer said with a shrug. "That's why I said 'God-willing.' It's your dream, so it's up to you to understand what it means. I'm just throwing out a wild guess."

Paula grunted. "That didn't sound like a wild guess to me."

"Well, if I'm right," Sommer said as a grin spread on her face and she looked at me, "you and I will be having a lot of conversations this summer."

Sommer and I were inseparable after that. Every moment I could, I asked her about God and dreams and spiritual signs. And in response, she told me all she could about her religion, Islam. She told me about angels and jinns and guidance and misguidance. She told me about the questioning in the grave and the Day of Judgment. But mostly she talked about the human soul and its spiritual connection to God.

By week six, I was ready to become Muslim.

"Are you sure?" Sommer said from where she sat on the floor of my and Paula's dorm room. Paula was lying on her back in her bed playing with her hair, pretending to be ignoring us. Paula had already told me that she thought I was about to join some palm-reading gypsy cult and she'd never speak to me again if I did. Luckily, John was intrigued by the religion and was now studying Islam on his own.

"Yes," I said, probably sounding too eager. But I couldn't help it. I didn't want to wait another minute. I knew I wanted to be Muslim—needed to be Muslim—and now was as good time as any.

Sommer clapped her hands together like a little kid and said, "Yes!" Then she said, "Repeat after me…"

I bear witness that nothing has the right to be worshipped except God alone, and I bear witness that Muhammad (peace be upon him) is His slave and messenger.

We hugged and squealed and danced around the room, and Sommer even had tears in her eyes. "I get so many blessings for doing this, you can't imagine!" she said.

"Can a gay person be Muslim?"

The question was so unexpected and out of place that we halted our giddy display as we both looked over toward where Paula lay lazily on her back still looking at the ends of some strands of hair. Sommer's excited expression faded to one of concern, and since she was sure she had our attention, Paula pushed her hair back with the flat of her palm and turned on her side to face us, her head propped up by a fist on her cheek and an elbow in the bed. I couldn't tell if Paula was being sarcastic or serious.

"What?"

To my ears, it sounded like Sommer was offended or something, but in retrospect, I can't be sure. In fact, given everything that happened after that, I know I must have read too much into the shock in Sommer's tone. Or maybe I was just projecting my own feelings on the tone in Sommer's voice.

I really didn't appreciate Paula using this moment to incite one of her silly, philosophical debates. Paula loved throwing out epithets at the most inopportune times, especially if she felt she caught you in a contradiction of argument or behavior. Over the years, Paula had been especially generous, to put it politely, in calling me sexist and racist. I was allegedly sexist because I felt that there was *some* value in keeping my virginity until marriage and because I had no problem with being a stay-at-home-mom one day while my future husband (whoever that would be) worked to support the family. I was allegedly racist because I honestly felt that White privilege remained a reality and, as such, our country having *some* exclusively Black programs and scholarships would be helpful to disadvantaged African-Americans. "That's reverse racism," she would blurt out in the middle of one of my explanations.

I hated labels. I really did. My tumultuous, bittersweet friendship with Paula and my love-hate experience with our deep discussions once inspired me to make the New Year's resolution to never call anyone sexist or racist. I would use those labels only for actions I felt deserved the label, but never people.

"Can a gay person be Muslim?" Paula repeated as she sat up fully. This time, I was sure I saw a mischievous grin lingering behind her curious expression.

"You mean gay as in..." Sommer said, clearly uncomfortable with where this was going.

"Gay as in a guy likes guys, and a girl likes girls," Paula said.

"Homosexual, you mean?"

Paula waved her hand dismissively. "Don't use that term," she said. "It's so archaic. It's like calling Faith a Negress."

I gritted my teeth to calm myself. Why did Paula insist on doing this? What did she get out of it? I wondered if this was a set-up to accuse Sommer of being homophobic. Because *obviously* if you didn't believe something to be morally or religiously correct, it meant you were a bigot. *Oh, puh-leeease*, I said to Paula in my head. *So are all non-Jews anti-Semitic, and are all non-Muslims Islamophobic because they believe these faiths to be "wrong" as far as religious truth goes?*

"Yes," Sommer said tentatively, as if sensing there was a catch. Apparently, she herself had gotten to know Paula pretty well these past few weeks. "But—"

"That's all I wanted to know," Paula said, flashing a smile at us both. "Because I think I want to be Muslim too."

PART TWO

After the summer internship, Paula and I went our separate ways. We kept in touch, but we had our own lives to focus on. I went to college close to home to be near John, and Paula went to college in another state. When we talked, which was usually about once a month, Paula talked mostly about her burgeoning spirituality and all the different Islamic awareness activities Sommer was organizing. Though Sommer herself lived far from us both, Sommer was active nationally in several Muslim youth organizations and ran a pretty successful blog that focused on sexism amongst Muslims and the need for feminist interpretations of long-held patriarchal interpretations of the Qur'an and prophetic traditions.

Once Paula had even called to tell me that I absolutely had to turn on the TV "at this moment" because Sommer was being featured on a CNN special about Islam's alleged oppression of women. John was due any minute to pick me up and take me out to dinner, but I was curious enough to turn on the TV while I waited. John rang the doorbell while I was still watching and I asked if he could give me a minute, and he stood in the front room of my apartment watching snippets of the show himself as he waited for me.

"That's the girl who taught you about Islam?" John remarked after we were in the car.

"Yeah," I said, smiling to myself as I buckled my seatbelt in the passenger seat. I was proud to have personally known someone who was so prominent.

"Good thing you only knew her for a few weeks."

My eyebrows shot up as I regarded John. "What do you mean?"

He shrugged. "I don't know, Faith. She just sounds a little too opinionated for her own good."

I smirked. "You know what Paula would call you now?"

He grinned knowingly. "A sexist?"

"And maybe a racist too."

We both laughed.

"Why racist?" he said, humor still in his tone.

"Because it's obvious you think Arab-Pakistani girls don't have a right to their own minds."

We chuckled, shaking our heads. It was a bitter joke because John was White, and he often said he felt reluctant to share his opinions about anything objectionable that a non-White did because he feared he would be labeled a racist.

"But I do agree with one thing she said." John's tone was serious.

"What's that?" I asked, curious.

"That people who are gay and lesbian have a right to worship God like everyone else."

I grew silent and looked out the passenger side window. The day I became Muslim Paula had asked Sommer if a gay person could be Muslim. When Sommer said yes (albeit reluctantly), Paula said, "That's all I wanted to know. Because I think I want to be Muslim too." Then she became Muslim herself.

More than a year had passed since that conversation, and I couldn't get it out of my head. What did Paula mean by that? Did she consider herself gay? But that didn't make any sense. In high school, she'd had more boyfriends than most of the girls we knew. Was this because she was confused about her sexuality? Or maybe she was putting on a façade to hide who she really was.

"Yeah," I agreed noncommittally, but I continued to stare out the window next to me. "We all sin. Nobody should be prevented from worshipping God just because their struggle is different from other people's."

"I'm ready, Faith," John said seconds later.

I turned to him, my forehead creased. "Ready for what?"

"To become Muslim." He smiled flirtatiously then added, "And to marry you."

I brought a hand to my mouth in surprise. "Are you serious?"

"If you are," he said as he slowed to a stop behind a line of cars.

"Is this your idea of a proposal?" I teased. "Asking me to marry you at a stoplight?"

"It's more than an idea actually," he said, smiling at me before turning his attention back to the road. "I want us to make it reality."

Married Life

John and I eloped a week later so that we could enjoy each other's company before making any official announcements of a formal wedding to our friends or family. Though I wanted to tell Paula, John convinced me that we should keep the decision to ourselves.

"What if she doesn't approve?" he asked one day as we lay awake in his apartment. "It would crush you, and I want the memories of this time to always be special for us."

"I think she'll be happy for me," I said, but I detected hesitance in my tone. Sommer had practically become a spiritual mentor to Paula, and though I wanted to believe that was a good thing, Paula's rants about male patriarchy in religion were increasingly more passionate than they were before she accepted Islam. I could only assume her views on early marriage (I was only nineteen and John twenty-one) did not mirror mine.

The mere possibility of hearing Paula criticize me for "dishonoring my womanhood" by giving myself to a man before I even had a college degree made my stomach churn in dread. John was right. We should keep this between ourselves for now. Besides, I was beside myself in happiness to be with John right then, and I didn't need anyone else's opinion, dissenting or otherwise, to make that feeling any more genuine.

"No it's not. No it's not!" My eyes fluttered open in the darkness, and I found John sleeping next to me, his breathing soft and rhythmic. My heart pounded with the same frustrated conviction that it had the first time I'd seen the dream. I sat up in bed, confusion and worry lingering where grogginess should have been.

The dream was unchanged. I had no idea what I was arguing about, and I didn't even know whom I was arguing with except that she was some girl with a faded red-heart tattoo on her lower back. I felt close and distant from myself at once, and the more I yelled, the farther the girl was out of my reach and the closer to myself I felt. There were black snakes and lizards coming toward the girl, but she didn't see them because she was so happy and content with whatever she was telling me. "No it's not!" I kept telling her in response, growing more desperate with each moment. And right before I woke up, I was in a green pasture alone, far from the girl, but I was losing my voice yelling at her though I knew she couldn't hear me.

"It means you're going to find the truth," Sommer had said, interpreting the dream. *"And after you find it, you're going to be tempted by yourself or someone you love to give up your faith, but you won't* insha'Allah.*"*

Unable to sleep, I tossed aside the comforter, causing John to stir in his sleep. I went to the bathroom then washed my face. John and I were scheduled to have breakfast with my birth mother at nine o'clock the following morning, so I really needed to sleep.

Was I getting cold feet? Was that what this was about? I'd asked John to come with me because I thought it would make things easier. But now I wasn't so sure. I'd suggested to John that accompanying me might be the inspiration he needed to find his own birth parents. Like myself, John was adopted. But unlike myself, John didn't have the slightest inclination to find his real mother and father.

"What if they're drug addicts or something?" he'd often say.

"So what if they are?" I'd retort.

"It's different for African-American families," he'd said once. "You all have closer bonds with your parents."

"What? That's not true." I don't know why, but I was deeply hurt by that comment. I guess in a way I felt that this was John's pathetic attempt to avoid facing his past. Unlike my own experience as the brown child of two White parents, John's outings with his adopted parents never incited questions or suspicions as to who his "real" parents were. Like my own adopted parents, John's were White, as was John, so people naturally assumed that John was their biological son. Apparently, other than close family and John himself, they'd never told anyone that John was adopted, and I sensed that in a bizarre case of wishful thinking, John believed that if he kept quiet about his true background, it would disappear. He didn't even want to accompany me when I met my birth mother for the first time. I suppose even that was cutting too close to home for him.

After leaving the bathroom, I felt a sudden need to read the Qur'an before trying to go back to sleep. I was still a bit unsettled by the dream, mainly because I could find no reason for having seen it a second time. I'd already found the truth. I was Muslim now, so what was I supposed to get from the dream this time around? Would my birth mother oppose my decision to be Muslim? But how would she find out in the first place? I didn't wear hijab, and I certainly didn't plan on telling her about my conversion, at least not during our first meeting.

I removed a copy of the Qur'an from a bookshelf in our bedroom, and I carried it to the kitchen, where I decided to put some water on for tea while I read.

"We have explained in detail in this Qur'an, for the benefit of mankind, every kind of similitude. But man is, in most things, contentious."
—*Al-Kahf*, 18:54

This is the verse that would stay with me as I drifted to sleep the night before I would meet my birth mother.

A Life Changed Forever

The door to my apartment bathroom banged against the sink counter as I rushed inside. I dropped to my knees in front of the toilet and hung my head over the bowl as my stomach heaved and the contents of my breakfast exploded from my mouth. I clutched the porcelain seat as I vomited twice more and gagged on the bile burning the back of my throat. I spat into the commode one last time before reaching up to flush the toilet. I collapsed onto the tiled floor with my back against the porcelain bowl as the rush of water sucked the putrid contents down the pipes even as the stench of vomit lingered in the air.

I covered my face with my hands and my shoulders shook as I moaned and tears spilled from my eyes.

"I'm coming right now," Paula said when I called her minutes later. I didn't want to tell her what had happened because, technically, my marriage to John was still a secret. But I really didn't know who else to turn to. After John, she was the only person I considered a good friend. I wanted to talk to my mother (my adopted mother) but I hadn't even told her I was Muslim or that I had found my birth mother—

81

or that I'd run off and married John without her knowledge. And I knew now wasn't the time to divulge this, especially after what had happened at breakfast.

It was late at night when Paula stepped inside my apartment and found me sitting in the dark living room, staring off into space with my legs folded pretzel-style in front of me on the couch.

"You left your door open," she said, playfully scolding me as she closed the front door and locked it. A second later light flooded the room.

I managed a tightlipped smile, but I didn't look in her direction. She put her arms around me and pulled me into an embrace, and I laid my head on her shoulder. The tears welled in my eyes again, but I blinked to keep myself from breaking down again.

We sat like that for some time in silence before she asked, "Faith, are you sure? Maybe there's some mistake…"

I drew in a deep breath and exhaled. I'd said the same thing over and over to myself the whole day, and I didn't even want to imagine what John was telling himself. I'd rushed out of the restaurant without him and took a taxi alone to my apartment. I still had a couple months left on the lease before I was supposed to move out and live with John full time.

"He recognized her too, Paula," I said, dejected, my voice scratchy as I spoke into the cloth of her shirt.

"But he was a baby when he was adopted. How could he even remember?"

I shook my head, but that felt like too much effort. I sat up and Paula released me so I could look at her while I spoke. "I was eighteen months, and John was almost four."

Paula averted her gaze. "But he's…"

"We have different fathers," I said, already knowing what Paula was thinking.

I groaned aloud. "Why is this happening?" I blurted, a surge of anger overtaking me. "I *love* him."

"But he's your brother, Faith," Paula said softly.

As if I didn't know that! I wanted to slap her right then.

Paula drew in a deep breath and exhaled, the sound painfully empathetic. "Maybe this is a test from Allah. I know it must be hard, but—"

"Hard?" I glared at her. "No, Paula. Getting through high school was hard. Learning how to pray was hard. Saving myself for marriage was *hard*." I shook my head and stood up, my arms folded over my chest as I struggled to keep my composure. "This isn't hard, Paula. This is…" My mind frantically searched for the term that could aptly explain my fury. "…f—ed up!"

I usually didn't use profanity, but right then I really didn't care. No words, not even profane ones, seemed heart-wrenching enough to accurately describe what I felt right then.

"Why would God even let this happen? Why did He make me and John fall in love?" I said, angry gasps between my questions. "He could've stopped us. He knew we weren't allowed to be together."

I clinched my jaws and balled up my fists. "This is so unfair," I said, speaking under my breath. "This is so f—ing *unfair*."

"No it's not," Paula said softly, but she wasn't looking at me. She was looking at her hands. I could tell she hated being in this position. She didn't want to be the one to tell me I couldn't be with the only man I loved. She didn't want to be the one to tell me there was no way for me and John to remain married. She didn't want to tell me that I'd saved myself, prizing my chastity and virginity all throughout my youth, only to give my heart and body to someone I was never allowed to be with in the first place.

"It *is* unfair," I said, raising my voice as I glared at her.

"No it's not," she said, raising her voice as she met my gaze. Her eyes filled with tears as her jaw trembled in tortuous compassion for me. She wanted to take away my pain, but she couldn't. I looked away.

"It's a test from Allah," I heard her say, but I couldn't look at her. Tears filled my own eyes as her words pierced my heart. I knew she was right. But I didn't want her to be. "You're being tempted to give up your faith," she said.

At that, I jerked my head around to meet her gaze and found that she and I were thinking the same thing. She apologized with her eyes, but I sensed she felt that, for my own good, I needed to hear what I already knew.

"It's like what Sommer said about your dream."

Moving On

*"Do people think that they will be left alone on saying,
'We believe'
And that they will not be tested?"*
—Al-'Ankaboot, 29:2

John and I eventually annulled our marriage, and we mutually agreed to go our separate ways and avoid communication with each other except online via Facebook and Twitter. But we kept even that to a minimum. A year after the annulment, John left America to study Arabic and Islamic studies in the Middle East, but I remained where I was.

Paula and I grew closer as friends, and as she had the day I'd called her distressed, she periodically drove six hours to our hometown to visit me. She eventually opened up to me about her own personal and spiritual struggles and admitted that she was in fact attracted to women, not men. But in high school, she'd tried to fight it.

"I thought I just needed to meet the right guy," she said. "But it turns out there was no right guy."

"What are you going to do?" I asked her one day as we spoke on the phone. I wondered if Sommer knew, but I didn't feel comfortable asking.

"I'm hoping for a miracle," she said jokingly. But I detected a sense of resentment in her voice. "Maybe I'll start a convent for Muslim nuns. You know, vowing celibacy for the sake of Allah and all that."

We both laughed.

"I'll make *du'aa* for you," I said more seriously, letting her know I would pray for her. "I know it must be hard."

"In a way," she said, her voice somber, "you and I are the same."

I grunted laughter. "I guess so."

But I didn't want to think about John. Even now, three years later, he still had a hold on my heart. I'd tried to talk to other Muslim men for marriage, but nothing ever worked out. There were times that my heart and mind would search frantically for a way for me and John to be together. I searched fatwa after fatwa, asked scholar after scholar, and read all the Islamic material I could in hopes of finding something, anything, to justify me and John getting remarried. I'd even found a couple of religious loopholes that seemed plausible justifications for arguing that, technically-speaking, John and I were not *officially* brother and sister—by law or Islam. And since our mother never married my father or John's father, weren't John and I technically "illegitimate children" who were not *mahram* (legal relatives) for each other?

"Be careful," Paula told me one day after I explained to her what I'd learned. "You don't want to do like that story in the Qur'an where the people were forbidden to fish on Saturday, but they put out the net on Friday so they could collect their fish on Sunday."

I sighed in agreement, but my heart fell in defeat. I missed John so much that my heart literally hurt for him. Why couldn't I just move on?

"But there are so many different interpretations of things," I said, desperate for any justification for what I wanted. "Maybe the laws forbidding *mahram*'s from marrying don't apply to illegitimate children."

Paula laughed, but I could tell she wasn't trying to be mean. "Oh please, don't go there," she said. "You start doing that reinterpreting thing, and you might interpret yourself right out of the religion."

"Maybe you're right," I muttered.

The Invitation

I hugged my knees and concentrated my attention on the parking lot beyond my apartment window. It was all I could do to steady my trembling and think of something besides the torn envelope and embossed card next to me on the crumpled sheet of my bed.

I was upset. I knew that much. But there was something deeper knifing at my heart.

Your attendance is requested at the wedding celebration of Paula Smith and Sommer Khan.

I gritted my teeth as I glanced at the folded ivory-colored card. On the front of the card was a faded red heart, and beneath the heart was the calligraphic quote, "It's about love."

No it's not, I protested in my mind. *No it's not.*

Part of me wanted to pick up the phone and confront her. I'd seen the link on her Twitter page to the article by Sommer entitled "It's About Love" that defended the rights of gays and lesbians to fully participate in Jewish, Christian, and Islamic faith traditions. But I'd thought nothing of it. Same-sex marriage was discussed in the article, but I would have never imagined that Sommer was implying that our "faith tradition" should treat these unions as Islamically acceptable.

"It's about love," Sommer kept repeating throughout the article.

"No it's not," I said aloud as I snatched up the invitation card from my bed and ripped it in half right through the faded red heart.

It's about Allah, I thought to myself, reflecting on the tremendous lesson I learned from my own struggles. *And it's about whether or not you'll accept Allah's invitation to choose Him over your desires.*

I Feel Cheated

Nina's Life After Islam

a short story

Nina faces spiritual crisis after converting to Islam and getting married.

~

UMM ZAKIYYAH

Nina was, in her words, "one of the lucky ones", and when she tells her story, she says the one thing that made the biggest difference in her life was having Fatimah as a friend. And the only regret that she has till today is that she didn't realize this blessing sooner...

February 2002:

Nina's eyes overflowed with tears as she embraced the women who'd witnessed her *shahaadah*—the testimony of faith marking her entrance into Islam. "We love you for the sake of Allah," they said. "You are our sister."

The following week, Nina's childhood friend Fatimah encouraged Nina to enroll at the New Muslim Class at the masjid Fatimah's family had attended since Fatimah was a child. Eager to learn about her new faith, Nina agreed.

In the class Nina learned about *Tawheed* (the Oneness of Allah), the five pillars, and how to pray. When she completed the class, Nina and the other students received a gift bag. In it were two books, the Qur'an and a collection of authentic hadith.

"This is all you will ever need," the teacher told them on the day they received their certificate. "So hold on to these. There is no Islam except what you find in the words of Allah and in the life of Prophet Muhammad, peace be upon him," he said. "Remember that, and you will never go astray and you will never be unhappy *insha'Allah*."

"That's not true," a woman said six months later when Nina related these words and how happy she felt that Allah had made Islam so easy for her. "You have to follow a *madhhab*. We are too ignorant to study the Qur'an and hadith by ourselves," the woman said. "We need scholars to explain it to us."

Fatimah laughed when Nina called her later that night and repeated what the woman had said. "Islam is simple, Nina," Fatimah said. "There's nothing wrong with following a scholar or a school of thought, but this isn't required in Islam."

"But, Fatimah," Nina said, her voice shaky with emotion. "What if you're wrong? The sister said the hadith says we have to follow scholars."

"Yes," Fatimah said. "But today people follow scholars more than they follow the Prophet, peace be upon. The hadith is about scholars inheriting knowledge from the Prophet. So we have to take from scholars only what is from the Qur'an and Sunnah."

"But how would *I* know?" Nina said. "I can't trust myself like that."

"Don't worry about trusting yourself, Nina," Fatimah said. "Worry about trusting Allah. If you get confused, do what you did when you knew being Christian wasn't right. Ask God to guide you," Fatimah said. "And just like He guided you to Islam, He will guide you after Islam."

But when Nina hung up the phone, she felt as if Fatimah didn't understand. *Fatimah might be ignorant of Islam herself*, Nina thought.

December 2002:

Nina was so excited she could scream. She quickly dialed her best friend's number to tell her the good news.

"Guess what?" Nina said after Fatimah finally answered her phone.

"What?" Fatimah said, excitement in her tone.

"I'm getting married!"

The silence on the other end of the phone made Nina's heart constrict in fear. But the feeling passed as quickly as it had come. Nina didn't want to be ungrateful for the blessing of Allah putting Ammar in her life, so she pushed the doubts from her mind.

"Wow, okay…" Fatimah said, her voice cautious. "Where did you meet him?"

"At the masjid," Nina said, excitement returning to her voice. "The imam introduced us."

"When?"

"Three weeks ago."

"Three weeks ago!" Fatimah couldn't contain her exasperation. "Nina, you can't marry someone you just met. What if he's not good? Did you ask some friends to meet him and give their opinion?"

"We talked in the imam's office a few times," Nina said defensively. "And that's good enough."

"Oh my God!" Fatimah said. "You didn't even talk to him on the phone or see him outside the masjid?"

Nina groaned and rolled her eyes. "I should've known not to call you," she said. "My *wali*'s wife said that people from your masjid think you have to fall in love before marriage. But that's not the Sunnah, Fatimah." Nina felt a bit awkward having to advise the one who'd taught her about Islam. "The Companions of the Prophet didn't date and mix with the opposite sex."

Nina heard her friend sigh through the phone.
"Nina, I don't believe in dating and mixing," Fatimah said. "But you have to do your research and ask Ammar some hard questions. You have let your family and friends meet him and see how he acts with them."

"My family's not Muslim," Nina said, annoyed. "Why would I waste my time?"

"You can't be serious," Fatimah said. "Do you think the imam would marry *his* daughter to some guy they met three weeks ago?" She was so upset that her voice grew shaky. "These people marry *their* children to people they've known for years. Don't let anyone make you think your family is worthless just because they're not Muslim. When it comes to marriage, that's when you need family the most."

"Look," Nina said, aggravated. "The *nikaah* is on Friday at the masjid. You can come if you want." She slammed the phone down and rolled her eyes, hoping Fatimah would just stay out of her life.

November 2007:

Nina was trembling when the plane landed in New York. As she entered the noisy airport, she whispered a prayer of thanks to Allah that she was able to return to America safely—and with her three-year-old son at her side.

The divorce had been long and bitter, at least that's how it had felt for the eleven months it took before she was finally granted a *khula'*, the wife-initiated marriage dissolution. Imam after imam and sheikh after sheikh refused to approve her divorce because they said she was divorcing her husband "for no valid reason." Ammar, a "student of knowledge", prevented her from talking to family and friends, forbade her from exercise or dance in the home, said she shouldn't listen to songs (even without music), forced her to quit her online degree program, and agreed to "allow" her to work only when he needed extra money. She told the imams and sheikhs all of this, but they told her to stay and be patient because "Ammar is a good man."

"You will not smell Paradise if you leave him," one Islamic studies professor told her. "So fear Allah."

"Even if your husband is a perfect Muslim," Fatimah said on a phone call Nina secretly placed when her husband had left the house, "you can divorce her husband."

"So you *can* divorce your husband for no reason?" Nina found this shocking.

"Of course not," Fatimah said. "But your reason might be that you fear for your soul if you stay with him. He doesn't have to be a bad man."

"Not in their *madhhab*," Nina had said, groaning. "I swear, I'm so fed up with hearing about this scholar's opinion and that scholar's opinion, I could scream." She slapped a hand to her forehead. "O Allah, what happened to just following the Qur'an and Sunnah?"

"Nina!"

Nina turned from the carousel at baggage claim and saw the beaming face of Fatimah framed in a floral-print hijab. Nina was so happy to see her friend that she had to resist running to her and drawing her into a hug.

'I Feel Cheated'

"I feel cheated," Nina says. And when she's asked why, she says because the Islam she learned before becoming Muslim was nothing like what she was asked to live after accepting Islam. "I grew so depressed that I wanted to leave Islam," she says.

But what saved her is having a good friend...

And remembering this about her religion:

There is no Islam except what you find in the words of Allah and in the life of Prophet Muhammad, peace be upon him.

So today, Nina counts herself as "lucky" because, unlike others who left Islam because of the teachings of people, she stayed because of the teachings of Allah and His Messenger.

Can't Believe They Did That

a short story

Upon her friend's urging and against her sister's protests, Barakah accepts a Muslim school's offer to publish her educational software.

~

UMM ZAKIYYAH

"You should really consider accepting their offer," Munira said.

Barakah sighed as she balanced the cell phone between her shoulder and ear as she finished typing an email to the editor of the university newspaper. "It's too much to think about right now," Barakah said, her voice exhausted. She pressed send and leaned back in her desk chair as she held the cell phone to her ear now that her hands were free. "I have to retake the GRE next month."

"Do you know what this can mean for you?" Munira said. "You can pay for graduate school."

Barakah laughed. "And if nobody buys the program?"

"Then at least you'll have an impressive resume. Do you know how many undergrad students can say they authored educational software?"

"But I never planned for it to be a CD. It's just some notes I jotted down to help children with reading."

"Some *notes*?" Munira repeated. "You have pictures, diagrams, and even *songs* in there. I teach at a so-called prestigious elementary school, and I don't even go to the teachers' resource room for reading. I go to your blog to get what I need. And the students love it. Even some of my 'slow' readers are reading better now."

"But it's my life's work," Barakah said. "I've been writing down these ideas since I was tutoring special needs students in middle school. It feels like selling my soul to just hand it over to someone else."

"That's why you do an option agreement," Munira said. "You give them exclusive rights for a year or two, and if they haven't published and marketed your software by then, then it's all yours to do what you want; or you option it to someone else."

Barakah was silent as she considered what her friend was saying. Maybe it could work. She didn't know much about the Muslim school that was offering to convert her educational blog into reading software, but Barakah did like the idea of giving a Muslim business the chance to benefit financially if it should become successful.

"But would they agree to that?" Barakah said. "I thought companies always bought everything outright."

"Not small companies," Munira said. "They need time to get funding and build interest in the product before they can buy it outright. It's a business investment. It might work out. It might not. That's why they work hard during the contract period so that you have a finished product at the end."

Barakah sighed. "I'll think about it."

"Just think of all the blessings you'll get for helping Muslims," Munira said. "Do it for the sake of Allah."

One Week Later...

"Please tell me you're not even *thinking* of doing something stupid like that," Rania said.

Barakah steadied her breaths as she walked rhythmically on the treadmill in the living room of the university apartment she shared with her older sister, who was in law school.

Rania sat on the couch thumbing through a magazine, her face contorted as she looked at her sister.

"You can't trust these people," Rania said, "especially the ones who can't shut up about all the stuff they want do 'for the sake of Allah'" She spoke sarcastically in a high-pitched tone for the last words.

"Well, Rania," Barakah said between breaths, trying to keep from sounding as aggravated as she felt, "there *are* Muslims who actually believe in that."

"And you think *Munira* is one of them?"

Barakah glowered at her sister. "I've known Munira since sixth grade."

"Barakah, stop being so naïve. Don't forget her uncle *owns* that Muslim school that wants to take your work from you."

"And?"

"She's not impartial."

"Does she have to be?"

"Yes," Rania said, discarding the magazine on the couch next to her as she glared at her younger sister. "Especially when it comes to you losing everything you've put your heart into all these years."

"I'm not losing *everything*," Barakah said, rolling her eyes. "I'm getting a percentage too."

Rania grunted. "But whose name will be on *your* work? And how do you know you can trust them?"

Barakah pressed a button on the treadmill to slow her steps. "They're a *Muslim* school, for goodness sake."

Rania's eyes widened. "Please tell me you're joking. That's about as sensible as saying, 'They're *Christian*, for goodness sake." Rania shook her head. "Muslims and Christians are *people*, Barakah. And some people are good and some people are bad. It's their reputation and good character that makes them trustworthy, even if they don't have a religion."

Barakah stepped off the treadmill and lifted her towel from the arm of the couch and wiped the sweat from her head. "Well, if I'm going to trust anybody," she said, "it'll be Muslims."

Rania sighed and shook her head. "Well, then at least insist on a one-year cap in the contract. That's long enough to see if they're serious."

"Of course," Barakah said, "that's the one clause I said has to be in there."

Rania pursed her lips as she looked at her sister, concerned. "Just pray *Istikhaarah*."

"I will."

Fourteen Months Later...

Who do you think you are?

Barakah's heart nearly stopped in shock as she read the email from Munira.

```
We spend all our time and money
on designing a cover to the CD,
and you say you're not going to
let the school publish it?
```

Barakah closed the browser window, and her hands trembled as she pushed her chair away from the computer desk.

"The contract expired," Barakah had told Munira when they went out to the mall together the week before, *"and I don't think I'll sign again to let the school publish the CD."*

Barakah thought she sensed a change in Munira's demeanor, but she couldn't be sure. *"I mean, I know they're sincere and everything,"* Barakah said. *"But all this time, they didn't do anything to fund the software. All they did was focus on a cover design."*

"Well, that is important."

"Yeah I know, but…"

"But what?" Munira glared at Barakah.

"I just don't feel like they're the right ones to do it." Barakah's voice was shaky. There was so much more she wanted to say, but she didn't know how to say it to Munira.

For one thing, the school kept prioritizing other projects over hers, and they rarely even made time to meet with her so she could express her concerns. But every few weeks Barakah would get an email or a phone call from yet another administrator apologizing to her for how busy they were or saying so-and-so was sick and so-and-so had to travel and so-and-so this that and the other—all to explain why nothing significant was being doing with the educational property she had given them exclusive rights to.

"I thought of the coolest idea," Munira told Barakah four months into the contract after Barakah had expressed to Munira her frustration with the school just sitting on her project.

"What's that?"

"I was thinking about what you said about doing something to really move this project forward." Munira grinned widely. *"And I found a professional designer to do the CD cover!"*

"Okay..." Barakah was thinking it was more important to focus on the actual software design, but she figured Munira knew what she was doing. Besides, the school still had eight months to focus on the software.

"That way, when people see the nice cover on the school's website, we can build up interest. We might even get someone to pay for the software design itself."

"You think so?"

"Of course."

Barakah smiled, feeling a bit more hopeful. *"Then let's do it."*

> "Then let's do it." That's what
> you said about the CD cover
> idea.

Barakah's head pounded as the cruel words of Munira's email wouldn't leave her mind.

> So how dare you say we didn't
> do what you wanted! You're the
> one who said we needed to do
> more for the project. If you
> don't want the school to do
> your software, then the least
> you can do is pay us the
> $1,850.00 we paid the
> designer. We thought we could
> trust you. That's why we
> invested all that money! You
> need to fear Allah.

Barakah walked to the bathroom and turned on the water, the throbbing in her head making it difficult to concentrate on the steps of *wudhoo'* as she prepared for prayer.

"That's why you do an option agreement," Munira's words came back to Barakah suddenly. *"...and if they haven't published and marketed your software by then, then it's all yours to do what you want..."*

> And don't tell me about some
> stupid clause in that kaafir
> contract you made us sign.
> We're Muslims. We thought you
> were doing this for the sake of
> Allah. Now it's clear you just

```
want to make a big name for
yourself!
```

Barakah's jaw quivered as she lifted a handful of water and wiped it over her face. Tears spilled from her eyes, and her shoulders shook as a whimper escaped her throat.

```
So you better send us a check
for what we paid for the CD
cover design, and the over 100
billable    hours    we    spent
working so hard when you didn't
offer a single penny to help
us!
```

"*Allaahuakbar*," Barakah said, proclaiming God's greatness as she raised her hands in surrender, signifying the start of prayer.

"Don't worry," Rania said as she embraced a weeping Barakah later that day. "I have some lawyer friends who can get you out of this mess *inshaaAllah*."

"But…" Barakah murmured between cries, her voice muffled by Rania's hair. "I just can't believe they'd do something like that."

Rania sighed and shut her eyes slowly, silently praying to Allah that everything would be resolved smoothly.

"Just pray for the Muslims, Barakah," Rania said, sadness in her tone. "Ask Allah to return them to Islam."

Books by Umm Zakiyyah

If I Should Speak
A Voice
Footsteps
Realities of Submission
Hearts We Lost
The Friendship Promise
Muslim Girl
His Other Wife

Order information available at **ummzakiyyah.com/store**

Read more from Umm Zakiyyah at uzauthor.com

About the Author

Daughter of American converts to Islam, Umm Zakiyyah writes about the interfaith struggles of Muslims and Christians, and the intercultural, spiritual, and moral struggles of Muslims in America. Umm Zakiyyah's work has earned praise from writers, professors, and filmmakers and has been translated into multiple languages.

Umm Zakiyyah also writes under her birth name Ruby Moore.

To find out more about the author, visit ummzakiyyah.com or **uzauthor.com***, follow her on Twitter and Instagram @***uzauthor***, subscribe to her YouTube channel* **youtube.com/uzreflections** *or join her Facebook page at* **facebook.com/ummzakiyyahpage**

~

UZauthor.com